D1138621

CHE

Please renew or return items by the date shown on your receipt

www.hertsdirect.org/libraries

Renewals and enquiries:

Textphone for hearing or speech impaired

0300 123 4049

0300 123 4041

Hertfordshire

522 650 72 3

CHARLOTTE PHILLIPS

I live in Wiltshire, UK, where I spend writing in between looking after my family, who have been taught not to notice that I'm rubbish at housework. I love watching American TV shows in my pyjamas and I can't live without coffee and cake.

http://charlotte-phillips.blogspot.co.uk/

@CharlPhillips

Meet Me at the Honeymoon Suite

CHARLOTTE PHILLIPS

Harper*Impulse* an imprint of
HarperCollins*Publishers* Ltd
1 London Bridge Street
London SE1 9GF

www.harpercollins.co.uk

A Paperback Original 2015

First published in Great Britain in ebook format by Harper*Impulse* 2015

A catalogue record for this book is
available from the British Library

ISBN: 9780008119409

Automatically produced by Atomik ePublisher from Easypress

Printed and bound in Great Britain

As this is the final book in the series I'd like to take this opportunity to say a massive thank you to my amazing editor Charlotte, who has bailed me out of more head-crashing-on-desk moments in the past five years than I care to think about. Thanks also to all the team at HarperImpulse . With HI anything goes really, in terms of ideas, and that has made writing for them great fun.

CHAPTER 1

Amy straightened the grey jacket with the pink piping, the standard uniform for the Lavington Hotel, London, still unfamiliar against her skin after only a few days' wear. She adjusted the name badge pinned to her lapel.

Amy Wilson – Wedding & Events Manager, it said in glossy black letters.

The M-word. How long had she been waiting to have that job title? Years of playing second-fiddle as she worked her way up from trainee via a string of provincial three-star chain hotels, doing the hard graft to pull together business meetings, courses, then later charity dinner dances, Christmas parties and weddings while someone else took the credit.

Now she was at the Lavington, the position of her dreams having dropped out of the blue into her lap via a word-of-mouth tip off. It almost felt like being headhunted. The Lavington had been left in the lurch when her predecessor had walked off the job without so much as a by your leave, and by lucky chance Amy happened to go way back with the Head Bar Manager here. They'd waited tables together one summer in the distant past. A word or two in the right ear from her friend and the job was as good as hers. To be fair, the Lavington did have its back against the wall, but that didn't detract from the fact that she was *ready* for this promotion.

Had been ready, in fact, for years. This was her chance at the big time. This was an up and coming boutique hotel in a fashionable area of London with its quirky décor and a sprinkling of celebrity guests beginning to lend it a bit of kudos. It was a world away from the motorway junction hotel chain she'd spent the last few years in, organising endless cheap as chips buffet events while the manager bandied the phrase 'squeeze that margin' about.

Still, she might have the badge but the job wasn't quite hers – not yet. There were hoops to jump through in the form of a three month trial period. Not that she intended to need it. She knew all eyes would be on her this weekend for the first wedding of the season, one half-planned by her predecessor before her swift unexpected exit. It was up to Amy to fine tune those plans and pull the weekend off seamlessly.

With enormous effort she reined in the squiggling butterflies of excitement in her stomach as she walked down the thickly carpeted hallway toward the lounge bar where a welcoming choice of champagne or fruit juice should be set up and ready to go for the...she ran a sensibly short, nude-lacquered fingernail down the page on the top of her clipboard...Pemberton Wedding.

Pemberton.

Her quick pace faltered momentarily as the name sent a curl of nostalgia folding through her. Here was that mental stutter that has the ability to stop you in your tracks when you hear a name that takes you back to the past. Not that far into the past in this case. It had been just over a year since Luke Pemberton had left her in the back of beyond that was Purton, Wiltshire. What had seemed a happy enough relationship that would one day be taken to the next level had been stopped in its tracks when he'd had a job offer that meant moving away.

It was only the briefest of mental stutters.

Amy resumed her steady tread down the hallway, secure in the knowledge that whatever Pemberton happened to be getting married here in the plush surroundings of the Lavington, it most definitely wasn't *Luke* Pemberton, formerly of Purton. Because Luke Pemberton didn't do serious relationships. He'd made that crystal clear when he ended things between them. He was a free spirit who couldn't be tied down – he had far too many ambitions and dreams to follow first. And when he did eventually decide to settle (probably when he was drawing his pension) it most certainly wouldn't involve the need for a worthless piece of paper.

Luke Pemberton didn't believe in marriage. Any more than Amy Wilson believed in happy ever afters.

Amy entered the quiet lounge to a comforting surge of relieved satisfaction when she saw the silver trays of champagne flutes just waiting to be filled and the platters of posh nibbles that were lined up at one end of the glossy bar as per her explicit instructions. A perfectly-turned-out contingent of waiting staff should be along imminently.

All she needed to do was turf out the dark-haired bloke in the jeans who was currently leaning over the bar and scrutinising the bottles on the backlit shelves at the rear. In one hand he brandished the hotel wine list, which he'd obviously swiped from one of the tables. Drink sales rep or stray hotel guest, she really didn't care which, she only cared that he was ruining the first impression for the most important wedding party she'd handled thus far in her career. Amy glanced around, frowning. The bar attendant was nowhere in sight.

'Excuse me, sir?'

She crossed the lounge at speed, eyes ticking off sparkling glassware and beautifully displayed flower arrangements as she went. She reached the bar as he turned to face her and wasted no time in pasting on her standard professional I-mean-business smile.

'I'm afraid this lounge is reserved today for a private function, sir,' she said. 'Coffee or drinks can be ordered in the lobby, or there's a second bar further along the hall.'

'You know you could up your game considerably by serving

3

a welcome cocktail,' he said, totally ignoring her. 'Fruit juice is just so heavy and unimaginative as a non-alcoholic option these days.' He waved a hand at the line of bottles on the counter. 'How about something light and refreshing like elderflower cordial? And straight champagne is so bog-standard and predictable. I'd do a twist on it. A Kir Royale, perhaps. Got to make sure you use Crème de Cassis, though, no cutting corners with syrups. Or perhaps a Bellini.'

He might as well have been speaking a different language. She stared at him.

'A what?'

'Champagne base again, but blended with fresh ripe peaches. Delicious and a real show stopper. Or you could use raspberries if you prefer.'

He had perfect chiselled cheekbones and blue eyes that creased at the corners as he smiled at her expectantly, as if in some laughable universe she would ever scrap the requested drink plan of the bride and groom on nothing more than the whim of a passer-by. She shook her head lightly to get it back on track. Her instincts were clearly right: bloody drinks rep. If she gave the slightest hint of encouragement he'd no doubt launch into his sales spiel.

'Look, you really need to make an appointment with the Head Bar Manager,' she said, knowing perfectly well how exasperated Conrad would be if she referred some random wine rep to him, but prepared to do anything to get rid of him, pronto. 'The Lavington doesn't accept unsolicited sales visits.' She had no idea if this was true or not and neither did she care as long as he vacated the lounge right this second.

He grinned broadly.

'Sales visits,' he repeated.

'I could have a quick word with Reception and see if they can help you.'

Anything to get him out of here in his tatty jeans and T-shirt-beneath-jacket ensemble.

'That's very kind of you…' he took a step into her personal space and scrutinised her name badge '…Amy Wilson, Wedding and Events Manager.'

She nodded, biting the inside of her cheek to stop a smile bubbling up. Hearing the job title out loud gave her an inner tiny squee of satisfaction.

'It's this way.'

She made a move toward the double doors.

Owen Lloyd gazed after her, amused. Having arrived early, he'd been doing a quick recce of the hotel bars before the party started. From what he'd read in the press, the Lavington Hotel was becoming quite the celebrity hangout, and although he liked to think he already had hip and trendy London Cocktail Bar sewn up, it didn't hurt to keep your eye on what the competition was up to. Now within five minutes of meeting the wedding manager he had apparently managed to inadvertently land himself a sales pitch. Who knew what he might achieve given another five minutes.

At the very least, she was extremely cute to look at with her Miss Professional attitude and sparring with her was much more fun than making a mental note of the Lavington's range of house wines.

'Shame not to have a drink first,' he called after her, not moving an inch.

She turned back to him. She had honey-coloured hair that didn't want to be pinned up, with soft tendrils escaping to curl around her face, and wide hazel eyes, currently sporting an expression of exasperated disbelief. There was a sprinkle of freckles covering her nose and a pink blush rising high on her peaches and cream cheekbones that perfectly matched the piped edging on her uniform.

He nodded toward the array of drinks on the bar.

'Like to join me? I could even get behind that bar and mix something a bit more interesting if you like.'

'No I would *not* like to join you.' she snapped. 'This room is reserved for-'

'A wedding. I know. You said. It all looks perfect.'

'I can't believe I'm getting sucked into an argument about drink choice. The guests will be arriving at *any moment*.' She flung an exasperated hand out. 'A wedding is, by its nature, a logistical nightmare. My position here hinges on there being a classy, beautifully welcoming atmosphere to get the weekend off to the perfect start. I simply cannot have random members of the public or salesmen wandering in wearing jeans and criticising the drink choices. Weddings and champagne go together. It's that simple. Gin and Tonic just doesn't cut the celebratory mustard.'

'I didn't say Gin and Tonic,' he interrupted. 'I'm talking classy, palatable, funky celebratory cocktails that get the guests talking. Champagne is so overdone.'

He reached for one of the bottles.

'Put that down!'

He spread his hands, unable to stop a grin. She was wound up like a coiled spring.

'Relax,' he said. 'Have a drink.'

'For Pete's sake, how many times. Even if I didn't have a gaggle of wedding guests turning up at any moment, I. Am. On. Duty.'

'So am I,' he said. 'In a manner of speaking.'

She stared down at his hand as he held it out towards her.

'Owen Lloyd,' he said. 'Best Man. At your service.'

'*You're* the best man?'

Oh just bloody *perfect*. She looked him up and down in his casual jeans-and-jacket combo.

'No need to sound so surprised. It's just a bit of partying with a speech thrown in.'

She opened her mouth to point out how utterly pivotal that role actually was, particularly in light of the fact the Lavington was hosting not only the wedding but also respective hen and stag nights for the bride and groom, but speech was sucked away by the sound of excited chatter as more guests entered the room. She turned immediately to greet them, pasting on a professional smile that faded as quickly as it arrived.

What the hell? She almost blurted.

The reality of the situation bit her squarely on the arse as she stared across the lounge. The champagne bottles, the glassware, the bloody annoying best man all suddenly melted into insignificance against the shock that fell through her stomach. She glanced back at her clipboard again, just to check she wasn't having some insane nightmare. Then back up. Nope, he was still there.

It bloody WAS Luke Pemberton. The wedding on which her dream job hung and Mr Marriage-Phobic from her past was the bridegroom.

In half a dozen strides he was across the bar and clapping an arm around her stiff shoulders.

'Babe! Long time no speak!'

She gaped at Luke in shock.

Somewhere in the course of the past year his accent, always working class, had somehow become more exaggerated. His reddish hair was in a thick mop style, Oasis circa 1995, and he wore drainpipe jeans, a slim-fit jacket and (most unbelievably) sunglasses, which he now removed.

'I hardly recognised you,' he blared, as if she'd had a head transplant rather than just aged twelve months or so.

'Me either,' she said. 'You look very…er…Britpop.'

From the corner of her eye she registered Owen Lloyd grin broadly from his place next to the bar.

'How the bloody hell *are* you?' Luke shouted. He gave her no time to reply. Everything was spoken a couple of notches louder than strictly necessary, as if he were addressing an audience. 'It's so great to see you. I'm getting married!'

He took a skipping step forward and waved jazz hands, as if he were making an announcement on stage. Amy blinked at him.

He took a step to one side and from behind him ushered forward a blonde girl with big hair and a slender figure that somehow coexisted with an enviable pert cleavage. Behind them, a slow trickle of wedding guests began milling into the room and heading straight for the drinks trays.

'This is Sabrina. My fiancée.'

The blonde met her gaze with narrowed eyes.

'Angel, this is Amy,' Luke said. 'Just someone I used to know from my home town.'

Sabrina's eyes instantly widened at the lack of competition and she offered a perfect white smile that could not possibly be natural.

'Great to meet you,' she said, holding out a perfectly-manicured hand, the nails painted a glossy shade of black cherry.

Amy shook Sabrina's hand politely and swallowed hard to clear the dry indignant sensation that constricted her throat. *Just someone I used to know.* Could he be more dismissive? Rising resentment mingled with amazement at Luke's clothes and attitude. What the hell had happened to the guitar-mad but totally normal guy she'd known?

'Are you still in the same job?' she asked him. 'Session musician wasn't it, for that recording studio.'

He stared at her aghast.

'Babe, you mean you haven't heard? I landed a recording contract. It must have been massive news back home.'

'I haven't been back home for a while,' she pointed out. 'I managed to land a job here. I live in London now and I'm so busy. I'm obviously not in the loop.'

He nodded as if it came as no surprise to him that she wasn't hip to what was going on in the entertainment industry. It seemed that he'd left her behind in Purton because boring old Amy Wilson didn't fit with his guitar ambitions once they climbed a smidgeon higher than playing the local pubs. Not that he'd bothered to tell her that of course, instead it had been all excuses about focusing on his work and not wanting to be tied down.

Sabrina excused herself and headed for the bar. As she watched, Owen Lloyd handed her a flute of champagne, his eyebrows raised in a vague impression of disapproval, undoubtedly because it wasn't some kind of uber-modern cocktail.

'Good news on the job,' Luke said, and she snapped her eyes back to him. He gave her a cautious half-smile. 'Sorry things didn't – you know – work out between us. Back home I mean.'

'So when did you decide that marriage was for you after all?' she said before she could stop herself, because he'd been so utterly adamant back in the day. 'An outdated institution, you said. 'No need for a piece of paper, you said.'

Luke shrugged, as if a total about-face was no biggie at all.

'It's just… *right*,' he said slowly, as if it was hard to properly capture with words.

She stared over his shoulder at the empty doorway and swallowed hard to try and clear the constriction in her throat.

The implication of that was clear of course, and she'd known it for years before she even met Luke Pemberton: Amy Wilson was obviously just *wrong*.

Things didn't work out because he'd been filling in time with her while he awaited a better offer. The real question here was, why was she even surprised? Being the also-ran was the story of every facet of her life involving the regard of other people. Past relationships, home life, work colleagues, in all situations she had been the warm-up act. She'd laughably thought that her relationship with Luke had bucked that trend a little. It hadn't felt like she'd fallen short because he'd made it clear that their break-up wasn't down to her. *Nothing personal, babe.* Settling down just wasn't on his agenda. Commitment wasn't a part of his psyche. Except it turned out now that with the right girl, it was.

She was the wrong girl. Again. And you'd think she'd bloody well be used to it by now.

'Forget it,' she said. Now she'd had the chance to collect her thoughts there was no way she was going to let him know she was remotely bothered. 'We've all moved on, Luke. I've got this amazing new management job…' she waved her hand to take in the lounge, now buzzing with guests '...the last thing I'm interested in is a relationship with anyone.'

He looked relieved.

'I'm glad, babe. Because it was – you know – fun. No hard feelings, right?'

Fun? She'd wasted a year of her life sitting in minging pubs out of misplaced loyalty. Fun wasn't the word she'd have chosen.

'Absolutely,' she said. She kept her voice coldly neutral. 'It never happened.'

To make it clear she was *so* not bothered, she came at him in full-force work mode.

'Right, my aim here is to interfere with your weekend as little as possible while at the same time making the whole thing run like clockwork. I'm on call 24-7, so if I'm not in the immediate vicinity then Reception can page me. Nothing is too much trouble.'

He nodded his approval and she congratulated herself on her professionalism, pleased that her tried and tested life formula, perfected over time, now held firm even in the face of this new confirmation of her inadequacy: the three no's, as she'd come to think of them: no emotion, no personal involvement, no distractions. This was a *job* and bruised feelings did not belong in it. She would treat Luke exactly like any other client.

'One more thing, Ames,' he said, giving her a winning smile as she made to walk away. 'If you could just keep schtum about our... *thing*...when you talk to Sabrina, you'd be doing me a massive favour.' He lowered his voice conspiratorially. 'Avoid the hassle, you know how it is. Cheers, babe.' He gave her a wink and a thumbs-up sign and sloped off to join the party.

She stared after him. So that's what it had been between them. Fourteen months of her life that she wouldn't get back and all along it had been a *thing*.

CHAPTER 2

There's nothing like a wedding – a celebratory gathering of people you supposedly know really well – to remind you that you may have been neglecting your place on the social radar.

He might be Luke's best man, but Owen had no clue who at least half of these people were. Then again, the Luke he knew from childhood who'd crashed on his sofa for a couple of weeks some months ago, seemed to have morphed into some kind of pseudo-celebrity since his band had been offered a deal, with a rock star wardrobe and a gang of hangers-on to boot. Owen made dutiful conversation with whoever approached the bar while he swept the room in vain for someone he knew, a member of Luke's family perhaps. The room buzzed around him with a party atmosphere.

It was supposed to be an honour, wasn't it? Your childhood friend getting in touch out of the blue to ask you to step up to the plate as his wing man for the most important day of his life. The thought that not necessarily meant to be the life and soul of this party, but at least to be *engaged* in it nagged at him. Instead he needed to make a conscious effort to keep his mind from wondering how things were going right now at his newest bar in Chelsea, despite the knowledge that he'd delegated all managerial duties for the weekend across his entire business. It could operate perfectly well without him for a couple of days.

Knowing that didn't make it any easier to switch off.

Unable to avoid overhearing Luke's blaring voice from feet away he picked up that the cute events manager also knew Luke from way back, not that Owen had ever encountered her before. He was sure he would have remembered. And from the look on her face the Luke she'd known was AWOL too. As he watched she glanced over at the bar.

The waiting staff had turned up but Amy was needed. Urgently by the look of the bartender, who was unable to fill champagne flutes faster than they were being snapped up by guests in full-on party mode. There was a measure of relief in being slammed back into work. She shoved the hideous sensation of not-good-enough to one side and gritted her teeth hard. *The job.* That was what was important right now. She was acting Events Manager here. The M-word was in her job title without the qualifying word 'assistant' for the first time in history. Yet another let down from her past could not be allowed to affect that.

As she'd honed her working ability, if not her whole lifestyle, by separating all emotion from practical arrangements, focusing on work was the most natural thing to do in this situation.

She manoeuvred her way through the throng of wedding guests and headed straight for the bar to check on the drinks.

'So you know Luke?'

She glanced sideways. Owen Lloyd was standing next to her, one elbow leaning against the bar, that same shrewd smile still on his face.

'He's just someone I used to know from my home town,' she said, unable to keep the sarcasm out of her voice. The dismissive way Luke had described her really stuck in her craw. Not that she had any feelings for him now. Months of throwing herself into work and a fresh start move to London had put things into perspective. She was over him.

She still had the right to feel affronted.

So what had happened between them had been a bit of *fun*. A time-filler. Her mind now insisted on trotting out a succession of scenarios that bore this out. He'd kept up a full-on social life with his mates while dating her, never really including her in that social circle at all. She'd met his parents only once, by accident in the street. There had been no meet-the-parents Sunday roast for her. They'd never holidayed together nor even planned so much as a mini-break. The examples rolled through her mind on a loop. Her bruised feelings were her own stupid fault for reading things into the situation that simply weren't there. His insensitivity however, was undeniable.

'We dated for a while back in the day,' she clarified, noticing that Owen was watching her intently. 'It was nothing serious.' Now wasn't that the truth.

The bartender was still refilling glasses and Amy moved behind the bar to help, grabbing one of the champagne bottles and inexpertly wrestling with the cork, imagining it was Luke's neck. The bloody thing refused to budge and she grappled with the bottle and forced her thumbs behind the cork.

'You'll take out one of the chandeliers if you do it like that,' Owen said, taking it from her before she could protest. 'Hold the cork and twist the bottle,' he said. The cork popped gently out and he filled a couple of flutes before handing it to the bartender.

'I must have loosened it,' she said irritably.

'You seem tense,' he commented.

'I am *not* tense. I'm never anything but calm. There is no room for emotion in wedding organisation. That's the key to making these things running smoothly.'

She would make this weekend happen perfectly for Luke as if he was a complete stranger. Which actually in some ways, he was. She still couldn't get over the image change.

She heaved an extra tray of champagne flutes from a storage shelf below the bar, forcing her mind to stay on task instead of doing what it wanted, which was to process this new and depressingly predictable slant on her past. There she'd been, considering herself to have one serious relationship under her belt, and the reality was that it had been no more than an overly long and inconsequential *fling*. Well what a perfect fit for the rest of her life thus far. She squared her shoulders and glanced around the lounge, noting carefully the lack of guests with an empty glass, checking the trays of canapés didn't need a top up. Guests stood or sat at tables in cosy groups. There was a general buzz of upbeat conversation and laughter. Things were going fine so far.

Guest satisfaction was always at the back of her mind, and she turned to Owen, who was watching her, and pasted on a polite smile. It occurred to her now that she'd dated Luke for over a year and not only had she never met the person he'd chosen as his best man, she'd never even *heard* of him. It was becoming clearer and clearer that things with Luke had, in his eyes at least, never been anything more than casual at all. Had she wanted to believe that she, Amy Wilson, could sustain a long-term secure relationship so much that she'd been blind to reality? She passed a hand over her eyes, trying to think straight.

'How do you know Luke? Are you one of his...' she coughed pointedly, '...more *recent* friends?'

The word *shallow* teetered on the tip of her tongue but she didn't use it. She began stocking extra silver trays for the waiting staff, holding each new flute up to the light and giving it a final polish before it was filled. Never letting the champagne run out was one of her standard rules. Nothing irked the guests like a badly-stocked free bar.

'Actually I've known him for years.'

She stopped mid-polish in surprise.

'Really?'

He took a sip from his own champagne glass.

'Our parents are old friends. We used to holiday together as kids, then we lost touch for a few years when I moved away. We met up again when he needed somewhere to crash for a while a few months back when he first moved up to London.'

'But you're not from Wiltshire?'

'Not that far from there actually. My parents own a farm near Bath. It's been in our family for years.'

Farmer? She looked at him doubtfully. The expensively cut dark jacket worn over a designer graphic T-shirt. She could pick up the light, crisp and definitely expensive scent of his aftershave. He didn't remotely fit her idea of the farmer stereotype.

'Crops?' she said for the sake of conversation.

He shook his head.

'Dairy. It's a family affair. My father runs it, my brother works on it.'

Owen could hear the stiffness in his own voice and made a conscious effort to iron it out. Family loyalty worked both ways. They might have felt affronted that he didn't want to join the family business but he couldn't stop the resentment at their lack of interest in his own venture.

'And what about you? You don't look like you're in milk.'

He grinned.

'That's because I'm not. Not unless it's mixed with alcohol anyway. I'm in the drinks industry.'

Her smile lit up her face. He found he didn't want to look at anything else.

'I'd never have guessed. Sales rep?' There was a note of triumph in her voice.

He pulled a mock-offended face.

'Please! After all the effort I made to wow you with my drinks knowledge. I own a chain of cocktail bars.

A surprised pause and then she smiled her approval.

'I'm impressed.'

He held her gaze firmly in his.

'Good.'

Amy's stomach gave an unexpected warm cartwheel that took her completely by surprise and she found her eyes lingering on

15

his instead of cutting away instantly. Heat began to creep slowly up from her ears towards her cheeks.

Just what the hell was she doing?

'Joe, let's have one of the waiting staff check for any empty glasses on the tables,' she said loudly to the bartender, to make it clear to anyone watching as well as to herself that she was still actually *working*, even if it felt an awful lot like flirting all of a sudden. She really ought to make her excuses and move away from this man with the crinkly blue eyes and the stomach melting smile. But it was somehow just so *nice* to have a tiny smidgeon of male attention thrown her way after today's reaffirmation of what her life experience had been telling her for years - that she was most certainly nothing special. Knowing it was the wrong thing to do – (which somehow made it seem even more appealing because where had doing the right thing actually got her in the last twenty four years) – she resisted the sensible urge to go and give the honeymoon suite a final check before the bride moved into it and instead got right back on with the conversation. A few minutes' ego-boosting time-out couldn't possibly hurt. In fact, it could even be seen as therapeutic. And there was still plenty to do here on the front line.

She opened the glass washer and began to move spent glasses from the top of the bar into its shelves.

'So you were brought up on a farm,' she said, wiping trays. 'How does someone make the leap from farming to cocktail bars? The two things couldn't be more different.'

He'd heard that exact sentiment so many times before. Was it any wonder he was reluctant to make family visits when they were underpinned by negativity? Not that he had time to schlep back home whenever he felt like it, you didn't build a successful business by taking time off.

'I know,' he said. 'My parents are completely mystified by me. They think I must be some kind of throwback because I couldn't think of anything worse than taking over the family mantle.'

He could hear the flip sound in his own voice. It was easy to make it sound light-hearted. In reality it had been anything but. He thought for the hundredth time of the flabbergasted response from his father when he'd first touted the idea of doing anything other than stepping into his shoes when the time came.

'It's a very routine-based life and a massive tie,' he said. 'Up at four-thirty every day of the week for milking. Massive emphasis on cleanliness so major daily hygiene routines to keep to. Hard graft that doesn't end until early evening and on top of that the constant battle for income with milk prices being driven down. It's not an easy life.' She looked slightly surprised at his outburst and he paused, aware that this stream of justification for his decision was still as much for himself as for anyone else. 'I'm not afraid of hard work but that just wasn't for me.'

'Hard work doesn't have to mean backbreaking physical graft,' Amy remarked, opening a carton of orange juice and filling a few glasses. She knew that only too well. The hospitality industry was no picnic. She was constantly on her feet, the hours were unsociable and she was dealing with Joe Public, who could never see the bigger picture. If they'd paid for a weekend away, or a wedding or an event, they couldn't care less if your supplier let you down, or a car was delayed, or if there'd been a double booking by an inept minion of a receptionist. Over Owen's shoulder she signalled to a nearby waitress to come and refresh her dwindling drinks tray. 'It can't have been easy to launch a business from scratch but you've obviously made a success of it.'

'The hours can be tough, I'll admit,' he said. 'This weekend is a bit of an exception for me. I'd normally check out at least one of the bars, making sure everything's running to plan. I've got managers in place but I'm forever on call.' He glanced at his phone on the edge of the bar, never far from his reach. So far it had been silent. 'It's been ages since I've taken this much time out actually. I kind of feel constantly like I should be somewhere, as if I'm missing something. It's ridiculous. I've spent so long building the business up that it becomes impossible to switch off. May I?'

She stared as he reached for the carton of orange juice and topped up his champagne glass with it.

'Bucks Fizz,' he said, as she raised eyebrows. 'Very eighties, but what can I do? You rejected my peach Bellini idea.'

He'd managed to elicit a smile, even if it was an exasperated one. He noticed that her eyes sparkled when she did that.

'Since you mention being forever on call, there's a hundred things I ought to be doing right now instead of chatting to you,' she said.

He leaned in close to her.

'So let's play truant together,' he said.

She smiled at him, tilting her chin up a little as she did so. It gave her a very cute expression that made his pulse pick up lightly.

'I'll let you into a secret,' she said, lowering her voice. 'I only started working here a week ago. The previous wedding manager was sacked and they needed someone to take over at short notice. I happen to know one of the senior staff here and they suggested me. Big break, right?' She didn't wait for him to reply. 'At least it will be if I can pull off the trial period.'

'You're on probation?'

She nodded.

'Yup. For a couple of months. They don't put the word 'probation' or 'on trial' on your name badge – it makes the guests nervous. But all the same, the job isn't really mine. Not yet. I know how the industry works. I need to make a great impression from the outset or the post will be put out to agencies before I can turn round. I need this weekend to be a raging success because all eyes are on me.' She straightened her jacket and nodded at him. 'And playing truant with you would be madness.'

He shrugged and picked up his glass again.

'Sometimes a moment of madness makes life interesting, don't you think? All that work and no play. And other clichés…'

He held her gaze in his own and her stomach gave a very slow and delicious, and extremely ill-judged flip. Probably because a moment of madness had absolutely no place in her life. Amy Wilson did not do madness. She did organisation, conscientiousness and hard graft. She'd learned at the age of seven that she couldn't rely on other people to provide her with security. If she wanted a steady and worry-free life that wouldn't be snatched away from her when she least expected it, she would have to get it herself.

She swallowed hard and took a deep breath while the stomach skipping subsided. He really had flirting down as an art form. Then again, she supposed if you spent the majority of your life keeping customers happy from behind a bar, flirting was probably as natural to him as breathing.

'Tempting though it is to just chat with you all day, I need to get back to it,' she said. 'I have to check in with the kitchen and make sure the honeymoon suite is all set before Sabrina makes her way up there.'

It was the oddest detached sensation, talking about Luke's wedding to someone else. As if their time together had happened to someone else. She glanced at the happy couple across the room, Luke looking like some kind of stereotypical rock god, a drink in one hand and his stick-thin model wife in the other.

Think of them as just any other random couple, that was the way to do it. Think rationally, not emotionally. Remove any partiality and just get on with the job.

She took a deep breath and turned to head for the lobby.

Owen experienced an unexpected faint twist of disappointment as she walked away. He was old hat at conversations in bars – it was part of the job. The key being to listen and let your customer talk about themselves. He realised as he looked after her that for once he'd failed on that front - she knew more about him after ten minutes than he did about her. How had that happened? Bloody hell, was he so starved of interaction that wasn't work-related that he'd blabbed his life story to the first person who asked?

He liked her. She was funny. And she was also work-obsessed.

Maybe that was it - God knew he could relate to that. Without any support from his family, setting up his business from scratch really had been a solitary hard graft. He glanced around the lounge at Luke's social circle, of whom he knew perhaps ten. His parents hadn't been invited. Ditto any friends he remembered from his childhood. The room was full of music industry wannabes, models and hangers-on. The kind of people he was happy to have as clientele in his bars. That didn't mean he wanted to pass the time of day with them. The weekend suddenly yawned dully ahead of him.

'Have a drink with me later,' he called after Amy on impulse. 'We can toast independent workaholism.'

She turned to smile back at him.

'I would. But I'll most likely be working.'

CHAPTER 3

A half-hour discussion with the chef responsible for tomorrow's wedding breakfast and Amy headed for the stairs confident that all was on track in the kitchen, and thinking through all the plans in place for tonight. This evening the wedding party would split into stag and hen groups. Sabrina and her girlfriends would spend the evening being pampered in the Lavington's lavish spa. According to her predecessor's notes, the groom had elected to organise his own stag night, off the premises, simply returning to the hotel at the end of the night. At least that was one thing less to worry about.

More guests were due to arrive tomorrow for the ceremony. Between then and now, Amy would be able to grab the occasional break but otherwise she needed to be on call the entire time in case there were any problems. To make things easier she was staying on site herself this weekend, in one of the sparse rooms in the staff quarters. Watchword: basic. Not a fluffy white bathrobe or basket of complimentary toiletries in sight.

Unlike the Lavington Hotel's luxury honeymoon suite.

The door was on the third floor at the end of a thickly-carpeted corridor with fluted glass wall lamps that gave the light a soft and smoky quality. No glaring fluorescent strip lights here. The perfect romantic ambience before you even got inside the suite. She pushed the keycard into its slot.

The trend for wedding weekends had changed the whole nature of wedding planning, not to mention hiking the budget through the roof. When Amy was a kid everything had revolved around just one perfect day. Before she could stop it her mind dipped back to her mother's non-wedding, all those years ago. Her seven-year-old self feeling like a princess in a pink frothy dress that she'd insisted on wearing from virtually the moment she woke up that morning. A ceremony at the registry office followed by a big buffet at the town hall. Cheese and pineapple on sticks just waiting for the guests to storm in. And a mobile disco. How very Nineties. And all over and done with in one day. *If it had gone ahead of course.* She shoved the thought back in the past quickly, before it could bite.

These days there were linked stag and hen nights and celebrations that lasted all weekend. Crazy locations or themes. An outfit to arrive in, a wedding dress and an outfit for the day after. Champagne practically on tap. The costs could be astronomical and any supplier worth their salt added a massive mark-up, because everyone knew it was all about kudos. Every girl wanted the perfect wedding day.

She pushed the door open and went inside.

Behind the glossy door there was no detail too expensive. She ran a practiced finger along the surfaces as she walked the room although Housekeeping had already checked for the slightest speck of dust. The mini-bar was fully stocked with a selection of celebratory drinks and soft options. The bed was beautifully made with tons of squashy pillows and crisp white bed linen. Flowing white voile drapes swathed the high posts of the bedframe.

It was impossible, given who the bridegroom was, to walk through the suite of gorgeous rooms without the thought that in some parallel universe it could have been her staying here. She almost laughed out loud at that thought. What had happened was inevitable, exactly what she'd come to expect from life. When Luke had moved to London to take up his new job he could have asked her to come with him if he'd wanted to. Yet he didn't. Instead he'd called it quits. Something better had come along and she didn't fit with his new improved life, she was just an unimportant part of his old substandard one. Years earlier, groom-to-be Roger had apparently felt exactly the same way about her and her mother. At least Luke had bothered to tell her it was over rather than let things carry on and on in ignorant bliss all the way up to the day of the wedding the way Roger had for her and her mother all those years ago, as they waited happily for their life to begin at last as a proper family. At least Luke hadn't been that gutless.

What must it feel like to see all this and know it was for you? To believe that in the years ahead you wouldn't be going it alone, instead that you'd be part of a team, watching each other's backs through good times or bad.

She couldn't imagine ever feeling that sure of someone.

Snapping the light switch on, she walked into the palatial en suite bathroom with its delicate floral scent. Sparkling clean roll top bath…check. Double sinks with spotless scrolled gilt mirror above…check. Luxury soft bathrobes and pile of fluffy towels… check…check.

Satisfied that everything was exactly as it should be, she turned off all the lights and backed out of the door into the hallway. Into the real world where magic didn't exist and spending a king's ransom on a luxury weekend was no guarantee of lasting happiness. And also straight into Owen Lloyd.

'Bloody hell, are you stalking me?' she blurted before she could stop herself. She'd practically walked into his arms.

'Now there's an idea,' he said.

Her stomach gave a dizzying flip. So the flirting continued. Not something that happened every day. Or any day for that matter.

He held up a key card as she pulled herself together.

'Taking a breather. People are still going strong down in the lounge.'

His deep voice sounded artificially loud in the deserted hallway.

'I'm sure they will as long as the champagne holds out.'

In her experience there was nothing like a free bar to give people staying power.

He glanced around him, then down at his key card.

'I think I might have got off at the wrong floor though.'

She took the card from him, conscious of the light touch of his fingers as she did so. Her mind processed details about him as if she had no control over it whatsoever. He was broader than she'd realised downstairs, and tall enough that she needed to tilt her head slightly to address him. His jacket hung open and his dark blue T-shirt picked out the colour of his eyes. She was pulse-jumpingly aware that they were alone in the plush corridor and he was just on the edge of her personal space. She gripped the keycard hard.

This was ridiculous, he was just another guest, and certainly not the first guest to wander the halls looking for his room. She needed to get a grip.

'You have. This is three, and you're on two. I'll show you the way.' She walked toward the lift just as if he were any other guest and not one that made her stomach do cartwheels.

The lift was worse. The double doors closed smoothly over a tiny enclosed space with plush walls and a velvet-cushioned bench at the back. She could smell the crisp citrus of aftershave on his warm skin. He leaned laconically against the velvet wall and watched her unashamedly while she tried to stop her eyes meeting his. Her fluttering stomach was made momentarily worse as the car lurched lightly downward.

She could have just waved him off down the corridor of course. But would that really *be* going the extra mile that the hotel management had banged on about at this morning's motivational meeting?

She stepped out of the lift and headed down the hallway.

'Here you are,' she said, coming to a stop outside one of the glossy doors. 'Room 205.' She handed him the key card. 'I'd better be getting back.'

'Fancy a drink?' he said immediately.

His blue grey eyes held hers steadily as her pulse hit the roof.

24

'Didn't we already cover this?' she managed.

He shrugged.

'I thought I'd keep asking until you say yes. Surely you must be due a break? I do have staff you know - there are health and safety rules.'

She was indeed due a break as of two hours ago. Her hesitation told him that much.

'Brilliant. Come in for ten minutes. I'll make you a coffee.'

He held the door open and waited for her expectantly.

Breaks were expected to be taken in the staff quarters. Taking him up on this would be mad. Then again, it had been a bit of a mad day, given the battering her ego had taken. Her usual sensibility clashed momentarily with recklessness, fuelled by the feeling of inadequacy that today had brought. She rationalised madly. So what if she had coffee with a friendly guest? Especially one who would be, by virtue of stereotype, in charge of tonight's stag activities. It couldn't hurt to get a bit of an insight into what he had planned. All in the interests of the weekend running smoothly of course. It could almost be construed as work if it wasn't for the flirtatious undercurrent and the vague sensation that she was really operating outside the rules here.

She squared her shoulders. Sod the rules. She was fed up with feeling like the reject. She was due a break and he was fun to talk to. It was nothing more sinister than that.

'Just coffee then,' she heard herself say.

She stepped into the room.

'What's the plan for later then,' she said as he poured coffee and handed her a cup. She added cream and stirred it slowly.

The L-shaped room was miniscule compared with the honeymoon suite but it was still three times the size of her tiny rented bedsit. Amy walked around the room trying not to think about the double bed with matching velvet coverlet was just out of view around the corner. On the desk was a laptop and a pile of property details. She glanced at the top one – a club for sale in Amsterdam. He certainly was putting in the hours with his business. She could easily relate to that. She sat down at one end of the berry red velvet sofa.

'Later?'

'Luke's stag do. I'm assuming you've been tasked with it.'

He scratched his head, mussing his dark hair, and half-grinned.

'I knew there was something.'

She stared at him.

'You mean you haven't made any plans? Booked anywhere?'

He shook his head.

'I just thought we'd head out somewhere…have a few drinks… maybe hit a club.' He held his hands up at her incredulous expression. 'Hey – the more organised something is, the more scope there is for it to go wrong, right?'

'That is the biggest pile of crap I've ever heard. And if he isn't standing at the end of that aisle right on the dot of 2pm tomorrow, I will hold you personally responsible.'

He laughed. A rich, deep sound that made her stomach flip deliciously over.

'I'm bloody serious. If this wedding has the slightest hitch, I won't get the permanent post, so no handcuffing Luke to lampposts or sticking him on a train up North. I will find you and make you pay. I know where you work.'

He held her gaze wickedly.

'That sounds interesting.'

She tried to think of an adequate flip reply, but unfortunately flirting wasn't her strong point. Instead she concentrated hard on her coffee in the hope that he wouldn't notice the warmth of the blush rising in her cheeks.

'It must be a pretty full-on job, organising a wedding,' he said, letting her off the hook. He sat down in the chair opposite with his own coffee.

She shrugged, more comfortable with the conversation if it was going to be work-themed.

'It is, but it's all about making sure nothing is left to chance,' she said. 'Double checking every arrangement in my experience catches most cock-ups before they happen. Some weddings are more complicated than others of course but ultimately you have to go with what the clients want, however insane that might be.' She paused to take a sip of her coffee. 'To be fair, Sabrina and Luke's plans are fairly straightforward compared to some. I've organised Wild West weddings with line dancing and hog roasts. I did a hideous pirate themed one where everyone dressed up, the main drink was rum and the background music was sea shanties.'

'Sea shanties?'

'I know.' She shook her head pityingly. 'Some people have awful taste. The point is, you can't let your own views influence that. Not that mine would anyway. I don't believe in marriage.'

The conversation screeched to a halt. He held up a hand.

'Hang on a sec. You're a wedding planner. How the hell do you not believe in marriage?'

She shrugged because it made perfect sense to her.

'It's a long story. And it's not an essential requirement, you know. They don't look at your CV and check you believe in magic before they let you become a wedding planner. It's a personal common sense choice. Nothing in my working life has convinced me that getting married is a way of securing happiness. There is no happy-ever-after.' She sipped her coffee matter-of-factly. 'There is only happy-for-now.'

Never expect anything and you'll never be disappointed. That mantra had been proven effective yet again today.

He was staring at her and she shifted uncomfortably in her seat.

'That's really weird,' he said.

She raised her eyebrows.

'Excuse me?'

'Your attitude about happy-ever-afters,' he said. 'You'd think someone in your line of work would be an incurable romantic,

27

not a total cynic.

'Has it occurred to you that my realism could be an asset?' she said defensively. 'Brides don't want some head-in-the-clouds ditsy individual who acts like a flock of white doves help her out with the organising. They want someone who quietly and efficiently gets things done.' She sat up straight, her shoulders rigid. 'Life isn't a fairytale. I know that better than anyone. I can't guarantee them lifelong happiness. But I *can* make sure the flowers are perfect and the toastmaster gets here on time. Once this day is over, they're on their own.' She paused. 'And good luck to them, because they'll need it.'

'Not necessarily.'

She flung a hand up in exasperation.

'No, and kudos to all of them for giving it a go. But in my personal experience it's likely enough to make *me* not want to take the chance. Why put myself through all the hideous stress of getting serious with someone when the chances are a break up is just *waiting* for me down the line.' She jabbed the air with an emphatic finger to press her point. 'I don't do emotional interaction. It just isn't my thing.'

'What about physical interaction?' he said immediately, knowing he was pushing his luck and not caring.

Their eyes met and held, and in the light flush high on her cheekbones he saw the effect he had on her. Heat began to spark deep inside him, a desire to take that further, to see where this could lead. She intrigued him with her spiky attitude.

'I think we're veering off-subject a bit here,' she said. She glanced pointedly at her watch and stood up, smoothing her jacket. 'I just don't need complicated relationships. Work is enough for me. Call it a life choice if you like. I guess I just want guaranteed results instead of leaving things to chance. And to be honest,' she pointed at him, 'you really didn't strike me as the believe-in-magic type either.'

He stood up and followed as she made a move toward the

door. Ten minutes had skidded by. When had he last spent time talking to someone and wanted to make it last longer? It seemed he'd become a bit of an expert in pointless small talk these last months. Amy Wilson with her off-the-wall take on life had given the day a lift. And it didn't hurt that she was seriously cute too, with her freckles and her hair escaping from its up do.

'I'm not saying you don't have a point,' he said quickly. 'Even when it works, a cast iron family unit isn't the be all and end all.' He couldn't help thinking of his parents with their single minded way of doing things, their agenda for his future that simply hadn't been up for debate. 'But when it comes to believing in magic?'

She turned at the doorway and narrowed her eyes at him, challenging him to contradict her. Sparks tingled down his spine and impulse drove him forward.

'I think as a life choice your attitude could have some merit,' he said. 'For example…'

His movements were slow and deliberate as in one smooth and delectable movement he took a step closer, curled a hand around her waist and kissed her.

His touch was expert, one hand at the small of her back, the other gently stroking her hair away from her face while he stroked her cheekbone delicately with his thumb. As his lips caught hers perfectly, her pulse hit the roof and her knees seemed to suddenly take on an elastic quality.

Only as he gently pulled away did she realise that her eyes had fluttered deliciously shut. She snapped them open.

'What was that about?' She tried to keep her voice at a normal pitch when what it wanted to do was come out as a soft moan.

He kept his arms gently around her, a cheeky lopsided grin lifting the corner of his gorgeous mouth. Her mind zeroed in madly on the caress of his hand against the small of her back, a dissolving sensation was tingling its way down her spine.

'You believe in happy-for-now and I'm all for moments of madness – remember? You and I are so alike Amy – too busy with

work to fit in anything that resembles a private life.'

His lips brushed hers in between words. He tasted faintly of coffee. Her heart slammed non-stop against her ribcage.

'Today, talking to you made me happy. Right now, kissing you makes me happy. I can't say if it will or won't tomorrow, but who cares because as long as I go into it with my eyes open, what can possibly go wrong? Why can't we have a moment of madness without the future complicating it?'

She could see the challenge in his eyes. A moment of madness? A fling? Amy Wilson didn't do things like that. She was the nice girl you could bring home to meet your parents. And hadn't that just got her SO far in life.

'I don't *do* relationships. Didn't I just get through telling you exactly that? Do I look like I have time for this stuff? I shouldn't even *be* here now.'

Her mind, carefully trained all these years to shut out all distractions from her life goal (to become the best wedding planner in the universe and earn a mint), struggled to maintain a foothold. It wasn't just the utter bone-melting deliciousness of his kiss, it was the idea of sticking two fingers up at the broken record of rejection that her life insisted on throwing at her over and over again. OK so she'd never been anyone's real deal. Not Roger's, not Luke's. Why not embrace for once the whole concept of *not* being the real deal. She was the warm-up act. She was Miss Right Now, never graduating to just Miss Right. So why not run with that and just embrace all that situation had to offer. Fun, desire, no strings, no stress, no inhibitions, no regrets. All of those things could be hers.

'This isn't a relationship. This is living in the moment. You don't want to think about the future? So don't.' He pulled her closer and kissed her again. Her stomach dissolved straight back into melty mode and all reservations were lost to the sensations he evoked in her.

And then her pager buzzed in her jacket pocket and reality bit

her squarely on the arse.

Just what the *hell* was she doing? Yes, yes, yes, a quick and gorgeous ego-boosting fling would be just the ticket right now after this new wave of inadequacy, but the bigger picture slipped back into view as she took a breathless step backward and checked the gadget. The extension number of the Duty Manager displayed itself on screen like a digital wake up call. She had one chance at this job. One chance. And she was pissing about kissing random guests?

She shook her head madly as if to clear it.

'I have to go.'

She was pressing the call button for the lift before his hotel room door was fully shut.

CHAPTER 4

The lift would be exactly what she needed: a calm and solitary minute or two alone to compose herself back into her poised work persona. It even had a mirrored back wall – she could check her undoubtedly smudged makeup and dishevelled hair before she checked in on the wedding party. By the time she reached the ground floor, it would be as if the last twenty minutes had never happened. As if she simply hadn't made the insane decision to cross Owen Lloyd's threshold, let alone to kiss him.

The lift doors slid open to reveal not the sought-after empty space but Luke, with his back to her, hands running through his carefully disarranged hair as he pouted into the mirror. She jumped.

'Ahahaha! What are you doing here?' she gabbled.

He offered her a grin and stepped out of the lift.

'I was just coming to look for you.'

She straightened her jacket and wiped her hands automatically across her mouth. Not that she needed to. He was so preoccupied with his own appearance she could probably have run down this corridor stark naked and he wouldn't have noticed.

'Really?'

'Reception said you might be checking the honeymoon suite over.'

It occurred to her that they were feet away from Owen's hotel room door and he could blunder back out at any moment. The last thing she needed was for Luke to find out what had just happened. From memory discretion really wasn't his strong point and all it would take was for the management to get a tiny sniff of what had gone on and the job would be snatched away from her before you could say guitar hero.

She grabbed him by the elbow and propelled him firmly back into the lift, putting some speed into her pace, as if she was extremely busy pulling his perfect wedding weekend together and most certainly was *not* snogging his best man.

As she leaned across and pressed the button for the ground floor, he pulled a sheet of folded paper from his inside jacket pocket and shook it out.

'Had a bit of a chat with Owen,' he said.

Her heart performed a cartwheel at the sound of his name and she leaned a hand steadying hand instinctively against the side of the lift.

'Erm, who?'

He held up a hand.

'Best man, babe. Tall, dark hair. Stood by the bar. Good looking, but not as good looking as me.'

Oh for Pete's sake. She failed to stop an exasperated eye roll.

'I always thought I knew most of your friends,' she couldn't stop herself saying. 'Never heard you mention this Owen though.'

He shrugged dismissively, completely missing the indignant point, which was that he'd given about five percent of himself to their relationship while she'd been giving it her all.

'Grew up with him,' he said. 'Top bloke. Hardly get to see him these days because he's trying to break Europe with his wine bars but he did let me crash at his place last year. Barely saw him even then. Guy works 24-7. No time for anyone or anything.'

Her mind zeroed in on the third party information. So Owen really was the workaholic he claimed to be. It wasn't just a line. She

33

felt far too interested in the revelation that apparently he didn't have a girlfriend or partner of any kind. It actually sounded like the guy barely had a *life*. She felt a vague sense of affinity with that.

'Anyway, babe, he's in booze,' Luke went on. 'And he's given us a few pointers on party drinks. Thought I'd pass it on to you, if you could just get it sorted.'

She stared down at the sheet of paper, her scruffy hair and make-up momentarily forgotten. So the menu and drinks had been agreed and in place for the last six weeks and he now wanted to change them on a whim with less than twenty four hours to go. She bit back the surge of irritation and forced her lips to make a professional smile instead of a grimace.

'Absolutely not a problem. Leave it with me.'

Changes to the wedding logistics she could do. In fact a bit of practical organisation could be just the thing to redress her own reckless behaviour and take her mind off Owen Lloyd. And while she was there she could get a clarifying bit of calming advice from her voice of reason.

She sped out of the lift and headed for the Lavington's wine bar. Conrad's territory.

'You snogged one of the guests? *You*? My you did take the going-the-extra-mile thing seriously.'

Conrad's eyes were amused behind his statement glasses and she put Luke's sheet of paper on the bar in front of her and clapped her hands over her eyes so she couldn't see his grin. And there she had been thinking a bit of supportiveness might be in order.

'It was just the shock of seeing bloody Luke again after all this time. 'I've spent the last year or so thinking he was a free spirit who didn't want to be tied down and that's why things ended between us when he moved away. Now it turns out he was actually just making do with me while he waited for something better to come along.' She sighed and leaned forward to rest her hot forehead on the cool glass of the bar. 'I'm a warm-up act, Conrad. It's the story of my bloody life. And so I may have acted on impulse a bit.'

She glanced up at him with one eye.

'So it's a jealousy thing?' he said.

She flung exasperated hands up.

'No, it is NOT a jealousy thing. I am NOT bloody jealous! I'm irritated that I could ever have been so keen on someone who is obviously so shallow. And I'm also extremely narked that somehow I wasn't good enough to be more than a fling but he's marrying practically the first girl he met since he dumped me. When it came right down to it, I was ok while there was nothing else on offer and he was playing smoky working men's clubs and stinky pubs, but as soon as he landed a better gig I was dispensable. What the hell is it about *me*?'

Prior to Luke the limit of her relationships had been the teenage school type. Short lived and based on who happened to be in her class that year. Luke had been different. Her first proper boyfriend since leaving college and getting her first job. Grown up and cool, with his guitar playing and his songwriting and his big dreams. They'd had a real laugh together. It was so easy to slip into thinking in the long-term. She'd been utterly clueless that in all that time he'd seen the whole thing as nothing more than a stop-gap.

'This has no bearing on you, sweetie. It's just down to him being a knob.'

She sighed.

'If this was just the one instance of it then I'd agree with you. It isn't about *him*, I'm way over him. It's about the *situation*. It's just another variation on a life theme of mine. And so maybe I wasn't thinking straight when I agreed to coffee. Which then led to a kiss.'

'You mean the best man snogs you and you ran with it for the ego boost,' he said, pretty succinctly she had to admit.

'Oh for Pete's sake, I should never have told you. It's not like anything's going to come of it. It was just a…mutual moment of madness.'

'Is that what we're calling it these days?'

'It was a one-off thing, that's all. No biggie. I've been living my life this last year or so without any emotional angst and everything works better as a result. I'm better at my job, I'm more objective about decision making, so it stands to reason that I can have a bit of a snog without it having to mean anything.'

She downplayed it hard. Perhaps if she did that enough the memory of it might stop dominating her brain.

'Yeah well,' he pointed at her with a bottle opener. 'There will always be a morning-after, sweetie. And you are still on probation here.'

'And the situation is completely under my control. I don't do emotional claptrap. I'm not about to put my career on the line over one kiss.'

No matter how bone meltingly delicious it might have been.

He flapped a dismissive hand at her.

'OK, OK, so you're on top of the situation. In that case, tell me more about Mr Snog. What's he like? Is he fit?'

She shrugged.

'He owns a chain of swanky cocktail bars. He's in four major cities in this country and he's planning on rolling them out across Europe.' And although she was trying not to think about how gorgeous Owen was, she didn't want Conrad to think she'd just snogged a total moose so she added, 'He's smart and fun. And really good looking.'

He clapped his hands together.

'I love him! He sounds amazing! Maybe you should make the most of the situation after all. I mean it's not as if they're queuing up, is it? Get this job under your belt and then go all out for a date.'

'He's really knowledgeable about cocktails,' she said, trying to ignore his go-for-it advice. 'Have you heard of a Raspberry Bellini?'

Conrad blew out an impressed puff of air.

'Bellini eh? I like his style. Between you and me champagne is *so* last season.'

'Good. Because the bride and groom have listened to his advice and have changed all their drink choices. That's why I'm here – to tell you to rejig your supplies.'

He threw exasperated hands up.

'Scratch everything I just said. The guy's a meddling pain in the arse.'

'Bit of a curve ball, bumping into your ex,' Owen said. The evening air was cool. The city beginning to come to life with streetlamps giving the pavement a mellow glow in the darkness. Traffic moved steadily past them. People heading for Friday night out.

He crushed the thought that he really ought to be working.

Luke glanced up from his mobile phone.

'Amy, you mean? Yeah. Didn't realise she'd moved to London.' He tapped the side of his nose. 'Keep it to yourself, eh? I don't need the grief from Sabrina.'

Eyes back down to the mobile.

The dozen or so in the stag night group waited while the concierge hovered, waiting for the convoy of taxis to arrive and take them into town. Owen glanced back through the revolving glass doors for what felt like the hundredth time. Beyond them he could see a glimpse of the marble-floored lobby with its velvet furniture. There had been no sign of Amy since she left his room mid-afternoon, not that that stopped his mind constantly returning to her. Spending that little time with her had been the best part of his day. Going out on the lash with a gang of blokes he barely knew held little appeal in comparison. The mantra continued to flash in his mind.

I could be working.

'I don't remember you mentioning her,' he said.

Luke stood up straight and pocketed his phone.

'It was no big thing,' he said, scanning the street for taxis. 'She had this big focus on her career, worked all hours, and she was really close to her mum. It was just the two of them. She used to watch me gig, we had a bit of a laugh, that was it. When I got the session job up here it made sense to call it quits. Nice girl though.' He nodded at Owen. 'You'd like her. Never stops working. Right up your street.'

Mercifully it seemed that Sabrina and her glamorous posse of girlfriends were perfectly able to while away an evening in the spa without any need for Amy's assistance, because she'd rather eat her own head right now than take her bruised ego into a room full of perfectly-toned models in designer swimwear. The spa team seemed to have everything under control and so instead Amy had the evening on call, which so far almost amounted to an evening off if you could ignore the sparse décor of the Lavington's staff quarters.

Her pager buzzed madly as she watched some awful late night chat show on the communal staff room TV. She'd spent the last couple of hours picking at a lasagne and trying to focus her mind anywhere except where it kept wanting to go, which was a constant looped rerun of Owen Lloyd's kisses. Somewhere around eleven she'd taken herself off to her temporary room, but no amount of trying brought sleep and eventually she got back up and headed to the staff room to make sleep-inducing hot chocolate. The pager, usually a total pain, was actually a welcome distraction.

She checked the number and crossed the room to pick up the extension. The night receptionist's voice was punctuated by odd slurring sounds in the background.

'Amy, I know it's late but can you come to the lobby? There's some kind of issue with the stag party for your wedding and I'm on my own here. The concierge is outside sorting out some kind of taxi problem. The best man's asking for you.'

Her voice trailed away and the phone clicked as she hung up.

Some kind of issue with the stag party? Oh just bloody *great*. In her experience the only kind of issues with stag parties were alcohol related ones. She ignored the immediate flurry of butterflies that kicked off in her stomach. They were obviously to do with hunger after the inedible lasagne and absolutely nothing to do with imminently seeing Owen Lloyd, who was *asking for her.*

She took a deep breath and channelled calm. It was after midnight now but she nipped back to her room and changed quickly into her uniform all the same. Professionalism never slept. She jabbed buttons through buttonholes at speed but didn't bother to put her hair back up. It was after midnight now and surely any guest in the lobby this late would be too drunk or tired to notice her up do.

The lobby was quiet and all but deserted. The receptionist nodded in the direction of three sofas, set in a cosy grouping near the revolving door. Owen was leaning against the back of one and he stood up straight the moment he caught sight of her. He wore a sharply cut slate grey shirt over jeans and despite her attempts all evening to convince herself otherwise, he was as jaw-droppingly gorgeous as ever.

Her stomach performed a tingling flip of attraction at the sight of him which turned into a surge of exasperation as she saw Luke slumped behind him on one of the sofas. He was dishevelled, messy and wouldn't have looked out of place in a gutter.

'What the bloody hell?' she blurted.

Owen held up placating hands and took a step backward.

'Hey, I didn't handcuff him to a lamppost or stick him on a train up North,' he said.

Amy leaned over Luke. He was completely out of it.

'Am I meant to be grateful for that?'

CHAPTER 5

'If I get him up to his room can you maybe organise some black coffee?' he said. 'He's thrown up. He just needs to sober up now and then sleep it off but he can't even remember his own room number. Maybe you could get it for me? I'm not sure he knows what planet he's on actually.'

She pulled an incredulous face. There were times when this job absolutely sucked, and this was one of them. She glanced quickly around them.

'Where are the rest of his mates?'

'Still out on the lash,' he said, pulling Luke to his unsteady feet and pulling one of his arms around his own shoulders. 'I told them I'd get him back here. There was no need for everyone's evening to be shot. He didn't seem too bad until he hit the fresh air.'

'*What* did I say to you?' she snapped in disbelief. 'Do not let him get pissed and ruin the wedding. Or words to that effect.'

Luke stumbled. She made a loud, exasperated noise and heaved herself under his other arm, glancing around the lobby. Where the hell was the useless concierge team when you needed them?

'Let's just get him up to the second floor,' she said. She called across to the Receptionist. 'Can you have some coffee sent up to Room 210? Strong and black. We'll take it from here.'

The woman picked up the phone as they began shambling

across the lobby. Luke was a dead weight. She turned her head away from his whiskey breath. Bleurgh.

'I take full responsibility,' Owen said, as if that made it somehow better. 'I took them all to *Loco*.' He glanced across at her questioning expression. 'That's my bar in Chelsea. Everything was great, Luke was dancing, everyone was partying, but we were short staffed and the place was heaving. I kind of pitched in behind the bar for a bit and then before I knew it...'

Was he serious?

'You *pitched in*? You mean you took your eye off the ball because you ended up *working*?' She shook her head at him in exasperated disapproval.

'Says the workaholic who's still up and on call in the small hours,' he countered.

They argued over Luke's slumped head as he stumbled between them across the lobby.

'Don't try and criticise me when you're the one at fault here,' she hissed. 'You should have kept an eye on him. He never could take his drink.'

The lift doors opened and they manhandled Luke onto the velvet bench at the back of the lift. He slumped in the corner, eyes closed. Amy stood up, grateful to be free of the weight and pressed her hands into the small of her back. She felt Owen's eyes on her.

'You look different with your hair down,' he said.

She avoided his eyes.

'Do I?'

'I'm sorry,' he added. 'I know I've caused you grief you don't need. I should have kept a better eye on things.'

She glanced up. His face was serious and her heart tugged a little in her chest. She relented.

'I've dealt with worse. At least you had the sense to bring him back here. Although he wouldn't be the first AWOL groom I've ever had to deal with.'

That special distinction was reserved for Roger Corbett, onetime stepfather-to-be, who in 1997 had decided that, on balance, family life wasn't for him. It would have been so much easier if he'd reached that conclusion earlier. Before his actual wedding day to her mother would have been good.

The lift trundled to a halt and Owen grappled Luke to his feet. Amy walked ahead down the passage with the key card and opened Luke's room. Tomorrow night, of course, he'd be joining Sabrina in the Honeymoon Suite. She saw immediately that based on that he'd clearly made minimal effort to settle in and was simply treating the place like a crash pad, which tonight it certainly was.

A battered suitcase lay open on the bed, oozing clothes and male grooming products. Luke's guitar case stood in the corner leaning against the trouser press and she realised with a flash of recall that it was the same old acoustic guitar he'd had when they were together. However far he might have come from his old life back in Wiltshire, some things *were* obviously beloved enough to take with him. She dragged the suitcase onto the floor and Owen helped Luke across the room and onto the bed. She leaned in to prop him up on the pillows and his eyes fluttered open.

'Sabrina?' he slurred. 'That you, babe?'

She moved her face in front of his so he could get the full effect of her disapproval.

'No it's bloody not. Drink this or your head will kill you in the morning, you muppet.' She handed him a bottle of water that Owen had grabbed from the mini bar. He took a couple of swigs and wiped his mouth with the back of his hand.

A tray of coffee arrived at the door courtesy of room service and Owen carried it into the lounge area.

'You want a cup?' he asked, putting the tray down on the low table next to the sofa. 'I'll give it ten minutes, just make sure he's settled. He hasn't been ill again so hopefully he'll sleep it off now.'

As if on cue a rattling snore emanated from across the room.

'Go on then,' she said, sitting down next to him. 'No point giving Luke a cup.'

'Not exactly running as smoothly as it could, is it?' Owen commented, stirring her coffee and handing it to her. 'The wedding, I mean. Sorry about all this.'

'They never run smoothly,' she said. 'There's always some problem or other to be ironed out. The key is not to panic. That's partly why I'm good at it.'

He raised his eyebrows.

'I don't get sucked into all the angst and emotion of the day. Like I said this afternoon, to me it's a series of logistical tasks, not a magical fairytale. I'm not about to have a meltdown if the groom gets plastered or the bride's hairstylist doesn't show up. I get things sorted. It's what I do. I treat it like a business.' She stirred her coffee. 'You must be able to relate to that. You're obviously unable to cope with downtime.'

'Excuse me?' He gave her a mock-offended grin.

'This evening.' She pointed at him with her teaspoon. 'You're meant to be at the heart of a night out with the lads and first of all, you take them to *your* bar. You could have gone anywhere in London.'

'So what? It's a great bar. You should come.'

She tried to deny the way her mind zeroed in on that last comment. That was *not* him asking for a date. She'd misconstrued enough comments in her time to know a throwaway flirt when she heard one. She took a steadying sip of coffee.

'Second of all, when you should be at the centre of the party, you can't stop yourself getting behind the bar and doing some work. You're a workaholic.'

'Takes one to know one,' he said immediately.

She smiled.

'Fair point I suppose.'

She leaned back on the sofa. Luke's heavy breathing seemed to be getting steadier.

'It must be great knowing it's *your* business,' she said. 'I've spent a long time trying to get on in my job. I worked in three different

43

hotels as an assistant manager before this job came up and in all of them I knew I could do the manager's job better than they could. It must be great to see proper results for the work you're putting in. Proper *return*.'

'It is. It helps that I love the business I'm in. I'm not sure I could be this productive if I didn't enjoy going to work every day.'

'Dairy farming didn't really cut it for you, then,' she said.

Her tone was matter of fact but Owen's pulse jumped at how right that comment was. The farm hadn't really cut it for him, proving against his parents' insistence that having something as a birthright and a way of life didn't automatically make you passionate about it.

'No it didn't. Much to my family's horror.'

She glanced at him with interest.

'Things haven't been easy,' he said.

'They must be pleased with how well you're doing now though,' she said, in between sips of coffee. 'I mean, you've built the concept up into a chain of bars. You've obviously hit on something that works.'

'You'd think,' he said. He toyed with his own coffee cup, not wanting it. He'd only suggested it to buy time with her. No point denying it. He'd thought about her all evening. 'To be fair, they never had a clue I was thinking of doing anything else. When I was growing up it was all *'when you take over, Owen…'* and *'keep this in mind for when you'll be running things…'* As a kid I never really questioned it. You live for the moment then, don't you, never thinking ahead. I got older and went to college for a business studies course. My parents really encouraged that, at the end of the day that's what a farm is after all – a business. So it was a bit of a kick in the teeth when they finally realised the business I really wanted was totally different.'

'It *is* a bit of a leap,' she conceded. 'Cows to cocktails.'

The grin on her face was infectious. He found his eyes drawn to her mouth again and again. The cute smile that touched her eyes with sparkle, the full upper lip that had felt so maddeningly soft against his own.

'I liked socialising as much as anyone at college. Probably more if anything because it gave me a sense of freedom for the first time. We lived out in the sticks, I went to a village school, my upbringing was all pretty idyllic. Lots of fresh air and being outdoors.'

She was easy to talk to. Easy to be with. It felt odd talking about the farm when he'd put so much effort into keeping it at the back of his mind along with the guilt he felt for leaving it. It was easy to lose the family childhood fun of the farm in the mire of bitterness that had followed.

'It sounds lovely.'

'It was great. The flipside of that of course was that I wasn't remotely streetwise. Then I went to college and suddenly I was living away from home in a big city. I got a bar job to help pay my way and I loved every second of it. I never got bored with meeting new people, it was vibrant and exciting.' He abandoned his coffee half-finished on the table. 'Around that time the market for sexy reinvented spirits was soaring. Flavoured vodkas had really taken off. I started my business on the back of that. I started out with a pop-up bar. You could hire it for events and parties. You must have come across things like that in your line of work?'

She nodded. 'Of course. Not quite as cutting edge as yours sounds though. Outsourced bars were really popular where I used to live. For fetes and festivals and local weddings, that kind of thing. Usually a couple of wine options, a couple of popular spirits, a beer, a cider.'

He warmed to his subject.

'I'd do a huge line-up of flavoured vodkas. Toffee, chocolate, cherry, you name it. I'd do a cocktail menu which went down a storm. Plus all the usual soft drinks. It grew from there really. Eventually I started thinking about branding and looking for premises.' He paused. 'And here we are.'

Amy returned his smile. It was hard not to be impressed by

45

someone who could exuded such enthusiasm for their work at… she checked her watch… gone one o'clock in the morning.

Silence fell between them and it was laden with tension. She caught him looking at her and cut her eyes away, only for them to creep back and meet his gaze again.

'Amy —' he began.

A massive honking snore from around the corner cut him off mid-sentence, killing the moment like a bucket of cold water. She put her cup down on the tray and stood up.

'I'm sure he'll be OK now,' she said. 'He's obviously just going to sleep it off. I'd better get back to the staff quarters, tomorrow's going to be crazy busy for me.'

'Of course.'

He stood up and followed her from the room, leaving Luke propped up against a stack of pillows, snoring at the ceiling like a warthog. More and more since yesterday Amy had begun to think she'd had a lucky escape.

She was acutely aware of him beside her as they walked together down the hall. He was a good foot taller than her and broad-shouldered. Her stomach skittered madly. Four doors down from Luke's room, he came to a stop. Her mind immediately treated her to a flashback of what had happened earlier today, the last time she'd come to this room with him. He flipped the keycard into the slot and pushed the door.

'Come in for a bit,' he said. 'Another coffee.' He held the door open with one hand.

Her heart began to thump because after this afternoon she knew exactly what that coded sentence meant. She could see beyond him into the room. To go in there would be a coded reply. A step in a direction she'd taken before, except that this time she wasn't deluded about the rules. He would be checking out at the end of the weekend. Whatever went on in there wouldn't last beyond that. There was a security in that certainty, no leeway in this for her to big it up into something it wasn't, the way she'd done in so many ways in the past. This close she could pick up the scent of his aftershave, spicy on warm skin. A half-smile played at his mouth. Slow heat burned its way down her spine and tingled between her legs.

'It's gone one in the morning and you think more caffeine would be a good idea?' she managed, buying time.

'A nightcap then. Or just a chat.' He shrugged. 'I'll be up for a while yet – my life is pretty nocturnal because of the job.' He held her gaze firmly in his and narrowed his eyes slightly. 'Dare you.'

Her stomach fluttered madly. Heat travelled deliciously down her spine and began to pool tinglingly at the top of her thighs.

This felt decadent. A moment of madness, he'd called it and her mind latched onto the appeal of that. She could deal with a moment. She could be Miss Right Now. Because those things had no aftermath to drag you down or hurt you. That was the beauty of them. She was in control here. No more reading things into relationships that weren't there. This was a one-off fling, something delicious and daring and something she'd never have dreamed of doing before. She knew what it was, knew it couldn't be more, and so there was no way this could come back to bite her on the arse. Why shouldn't she have this night? They were both single and no one else need ever know.

Her mind continued to justify her actions as she walked past him into his hotel room.

CHAPTER 6

As she stepped over the threshold she knew there would be no coffee, nor any other drink for that matter.

He stepped into the room after her and caught her around the waist from behind as he kicked the door shut. Tugging her back against him, he swept the sheaf of her hair to one side with his free hand, exposing the nape of her neck. She felt the whisper of his breath against her skin, her senses slowly enveloped by the scent of him, the citrus of his aftershave, the musk of his warm skin. When he pressed his mouth hard against the side of her throat, the sensation was of light-headedness. Dizzying heat curled down her legs, making her feel weak. Her body, driven entirely by the unfamiliar physical sensations he evoked in her, was hungry for more. She seemed to have lost the capability of rational thought in favour of following every tiny move he made with her mind's eye.

Leaning back against him she was deliciously aware of how broad he was, his arms strong as they encircled her. He slid his hands beneath her T-shirt, tugging it upwards and over her head, casting it to the floor and instantly returning to caress her breasts.

She sent up silent thanks that she was wearing underwear from the mediocre section of her knicker drawer. Could have been better – one of the few silk and lace delicate sets she owned would have been nice – but it could also have been much, much worse. Her underwear repertoire also included a myriad of greying T-shirt bras and comfy big knickers.

Note to self, Amy: If you are now entering the moment-of-madness phase of your romantic life, a knicker drawer overhaul could be in order.

Thoughts of underwear choice disappeared like smoke as he turned her gently to face him, tangled a hand in her hair and tilted her head to kiss her. Not the tender, soft kiss she'd been replaying on a loop in her head since this afternoon but a hard, deep, intense kiss. An opportunity to explore and taste and feel her. With a single expert twist of his fingers, her bra was unclasped, and his sigh of satisfaction as he cupped her naked breasts in his hands sent an exquisite thrill skittering through her. He caught her nipples tightly between his fingers and softly brushed their hard tips until her stomach felt like it was dissolving.

Shaky fingers found the buttons of his shirt. She undid them one by one, by feel, not wanting to break the kiss for an instant. Then her hands were sliding over the smooth skin of his chest, taut with muscle. Wanting more, gaining momentum as more and more of her senses were taken over by him, she reached for the button of his jeans and tugged.

She was driving this as much as he was now, and it thrilled Owen to the core after the tentative shyness of the first moments with her. She pulled his jeans lower until he could kick them away and then her fingers were sliding softly over him, tracing the length of his erection, and he thought he might explode. Before he could lose control he picked her up and carried her against him, the smooth flat length of her torso against his, the push of her firm breasts against his chest. She curled her legs around his back and her arms around his neck, her fingers sinking into his hair. Half a dozen strides across the room to his bed and then he lowered her against the pillows. Playing for time, getting his own desire back under some measure of control, he trailed slow, exploring kisses down from her neck, over her firm breasts, finding the stiff peaks of her nipples and sucking gently as she arched her back deliciously.

For her, sex had never been this hot, this impulsive, this driven exclusively by the instinct of the moment. As his mouth crept lower she tangled a hand instinctively in his hair, her mind following as he traced her navel with his tongue, moving still lower she sucked in a soft gasp as his breath warmed the very core of her. Slow, deliberate strokes of his tongue circled her most sensitive spot. She let her mind linger exquisitely in this moment alone, an isolated spot in time, no thoughts encroaching about what this meant, what it could be. It didn't mean anything, it wasn't going to *be* anything other than this moment. The sensation was liberating, uninhibiting. As he slid two fingers slowly inside her and found her rhythm she clutched at his hair, riding the wave of delicious sensation until she flew over the edge, soft moans leaving her lips.

A moment to catch her breath and then he loomed gently above her, she felt his erection rock hard for a moment against her core and then with slow deliberateness he took her. She rolled her head deliciously back as he moved in slow, delectable strokes, finding his own pace and then slowly climbing. She curled her legs around his back, fingernails raking his shoulders as they moved together for a long time. As she reached that plateau again his hands were tangled in her hair, his thrusts hard and fast until she cried out her pleasure at the ceiling. In the soft gasp of his breath against her neck and the clutch of his hands she felt him reach his own climax right beside her.

Amy's first thought when as her eyes skittered open was to wonder why the hell the rhythmic bleeping of her watch alarm wasn't coming from her wrist. Instead the sound blared from some random corner of the room. She wasn't wearing it.

She wasn't actually wearing anything.

Her second thought was that the bed was much too firm to be staff-quality. The sheets were crisper and the pillows were plumper. The furnishings in the staff quarters at the Lavington were basically cast-offs from the hotel itself that were roughly one step away from being lobbed in a skip. The mattress in the staff bedroom she was meant to be occupying had probably been slept on by thousands of Lavington guests before she ever got to it. It was a thought she'd tried not to dwell on the previous evening. As it happened she needn't have worried. She'd slept somewhere else entirely.

Then a bleary voice spoke out of the darkness next to her and she nearly hit the ceiling in shock.

'Bloody hell it's a bit early for an alarm isn't it? Half past five.'

Her sleep-dulled memory woke up like a shot. Scrambling out of bed in the pitch darkness, she followed the sound of the alarm, dragging the sheet along with her by clamping it against her breasts with one arm. She heard his yelp of protest as he attempted to hang on to it and then the sheet pulled free as he gave up. She found a pile of garments on the floor and groped through them, the alarm getting louder. At last she snatched it up triumphantly and pressed the off button.

The bedside light clicked on.

She turned back towards the bed, blinking like an owl in the sudden glare. Owen Lloyd was lying back against the headboard stark naked except for a strategically placed pillow. Even after the previous night out on the lash followed by what had gone on between them – warmth began to creep upward from her neck as the memory of that began to kick in – he looked utterly gorgeous. Whereas she was draped in a sheet, sprawled on the floor in the middle of a random pile of clothes, and from the burning sensation in her cheeks she knew she was bright tomato red from neck to hairline.

'I liked it better with the light off,' she said.

'Come back to bed.' He pulled himself up on one elbow, watching her. 'It's early. You've got loads of time.'

She ignored him, scrambling to her feet, dragging the sheet with her and holding it awkwardly under her arms while she wriggled back into her creased and crumpled uniform. She avoided his gaze like a blushing teenager on a public beach. All the while the previous evening crashed back into her mind in wave after wave of shocking images.

Only now did she realise quite how completely bumping into Luke again had knocked her ego. The Amy Wilson of even two days ago would never – repeat *never* – have jumped into bed with someone she met for the first time that same day. Amy Wilson chose her relationships carefully – *ergo* she'd had hardly any of them. They needed to have some kind of potential, some kind of staying power, for her to invest herself in them. Even if that potential turned out to be only in her mind. In the past she'd epically failed to separate the emotional from the physical in her dealings with men. As a result the situation with Luke had been totally distorted, each of them coming at it with a totally different agenda, she believing it had longevity, he making do until something better came along.

On the back of that discovery, her normal set of standards had been knocked completely off-kilter.

Clearly last night's moment-of-madness rationale could hold its own in the cold light of the very early morning, only as long as she stuck to that same theme going forward. The idea that she could do whatever she wanted, enjoy one night with Owen, worked as long as she went into it on a *physical* basis only and took it for what it was. No room for emotion and therefore no room for rejection. She would walk away this morning and never look back.

As long as word didn't reach the management of her little adventure of course.

A nauseating tendril of dread twisted through her chest as she thought exactly what she'd laid on the line here. It might have seemed like a snap inconsequential decision last night, the hint of danger about it making the decision to enter his room seem even sexier. In the depths of the night with only a skeleton staff and all the guests tucked up in bed, a hint had been the limit of it.

She hadn't thought as far as falling asleep next to him. At getting on for six in the morning, the hotel would be *alive* with staff. Chambermaids, waiting staff, the concierge team at full pelt as they shifted luggage down the corridors for checking in and out. Hotel staff sleeping with the guest was a line that simply wasn't crossed if you valued your job. Instant dismissal would follow. Lavington legend spoke of a guest services assistant who'd slept with a celebrity tennis star guest and had been practically thrown out on the pavement.

She'd put the job of her dreams on the line here because she'd been feeling a bit low about her past rejection-filled life. What a total muppet she really was.

Getting from here to the staff quarters without being seen in her dishevelled state would be like running the gauntlet, and it leached any hint of latent sexiness from the room. She took a deep breath and ran again with last night's emotion free rationale. No time now for regrets or self-hatred – they wouldn't secure her the manager's role. Instead she took immediate refuge in the practical. She could do thoughts and feelings about this monumental cock-up on Monday night, perhaps, when the wedding was over and the entire party – including Owen Lloyd - had checked out of her life for good.

'Breakfast is served from seven o'clock,' she said loudly. 'I'll have to be on hand in case the wedding guests need anything or have any last minute issues. The chairs need to be lined up in the ballroom ready for the ceremony. The florist gets here at nine and I'll be double checking the flowers. Tables need to be arranged and dressed. Oh and some meddling pain in the arse changed all the celebratory drinks options so I'll be checking in with the Chief Bar Manager to make sure he's on top of that.' The thought of what Conrad would say when she filled him in on what she'd done now made her head spin and not in a good way. 'In short, every minute of the day ahead is spoken for. So no. I don't have time to come back to bed.'

Owen pulled himself up into a sitting position. Firm muscle rippled his body and her eyes stuttered for a second on the gorgeous view. She snapped her gaze away like a misbehaving child and headed for the door.

'I'll catch up with you later then,' he called after her.

In the course of running the gauntlet down the corridors of the Lavington and back to the staff quarters it felt like she aged five years. Every corner she turned seemed to have a chambermaid lurking behind it or a breakfast-toting room service minion. She double-backed on herself three times, took the back stairs instead of the lift and at last legged it into her staff bedroom completely out of breath.

This was what you got for moments of madness. There was a reason why she'd focused so hard on cold practicality these last months. Practicality got you places with no margin for screwing up. And if she'd thought to put in place a practical exit strategy before having her emotion free mad moment with Owen last night, there wouldn't be any of this morning after stress.

This morning's fluster was *only* down to that, she insisted to herself, just the stress of realising what she'd done and then getting back to her room unseen. It had absolutely nothing whatsoever to do with any feelings she might be experiencing about Owen Lloyd. Moments of madness did not have room for feelings, that was the whole bloody point of them.

The plan now was to get right back into immediate work mode, leave the crazy moment behind her and hope to hell that he would do the same.

There was absolutely zero point going back to sleep when your body was on standby for a rerun of the previous night's activities and your partner made an exit that would hold its own against an Olympic sprinter. Watching her get dressed with her hair bed-messy and the glimpses of her peaches and cream skin was enough to get Owen seriously hot, right up until the point at which she legged it out of the room.

He might actually have been a bit offended at the fact she couldn't get away fast enough, if there wasn't a big rational chunk of his brain telling him her disappearance was a complication-busting gift. He had no desire to get close enough to anyone that they might feel they had a *stake* in his life, no matter how small. A morning-after swift exit was, in that sense, just the ticket.

He'd be checking out of here this time tomorrow and between then and now were a myriad of best man duties, not least of which was the not insignificant challenge of getting Luke to look and behave as if he was sparkling fresh instead of hung way over. Twenty-four hours and he'd never see Amy Wilson again.

For some reason, the expected sense of relief that thought should bring just wasn't coming through for him right now.

CHAPTER 7

An hour since she'd made it back to her room and Amy was in a fresh Lavington uniform, name badge in place, hair neatly pinned up, concealer under her eyes to hide the shadows, and heading away from the staff meeting where she'd confirmed with a confident smile that all details of today's wedding were under her absolute and capable control.

The smile slipped from place the moment she left the meeting room.

She squeezed her eyes shut and tried to think straight. On balance she'd probably managed less than three hours sleep and was pretty much operating on caffeine and determination right now. The day ahead was filled with hundreds of tiny details, all of which had to be perfect. She gritted her teeth hard as she headed for the honeymoon suite to check the bride was enjoying a perfectly cooked champagne breakfast, as per the explicit instructions Amy had given the kitchen. Sabrina, after an evening of healthy food and pampering followed by an early night, looked as fresh as a daisy in her Lavington Hotel fluffy bathrobe, her skin dewy and glowing as she helped herself to fresh fruit and muesli from the groaning silver breakfast trolley. Amy hoped she knew what she was letting herself in for.

Immediately afterward she swept downstairs to the dining

room. Onto the next task, then the next… Showing her face at breakfast would be a good starting point. After that she would take it step by step. She'd spent too long waiting for this opportunity to screw it up because she was too bloody tired.

Back to work, that was the thing. Get on with the day ahead as if nothing had ever happened and surely Owen Lloyd would do the same. What had he said? *Dare you.* Last night had been a fun one-off. To expect more would be to disregard the conclusion that had been reaffirmed to her over and over again, that the only true security in life was the kind you made for yourself.

Surely it wouldn't be too hard to keep Owen at arm's length today. It wasn't as if he didn't have responsibilities himself. He was the best man, after all. With any luck he would be up in Luke's room right now, standing him under the shower and making sure he was fully sober before Sabrina clapped eyes on him and called the whole thing off.

It wasn't just the sex, although let's face it, she was going to have her work cut out today trying to keep her mind wandering back to the deliciousness of it. Sex in her experience was not like that. In her experience it wasn't something instinctive and adventurous. It wasn't a laugh. It was more of an add-on. Once she'd been out with Luke for a couple of months it became something of a standard next step. In the same way she had supposed that moving in together might reasonably follow at some point. Perfectly enjoyable but not something that blew her away like this did.

She gave herself a mental shake and tried to squash sex from her mind in general. Not least because there was something *so* wrong about recalling sex with the bridegroom of today's wedding. *Eew.*

It wasn't just the sex. It was the way he'd held her, the easiness of talking to him and being with him, not just the physical side of it. When had she ever felt so comfortable, when had any guy listened to her and actually seemed interested in what she had to say?

And there was absolutely no point in this train of thought. Owen ran a chain of cocktail bars. Could there *be* a profession that lent itself more to casual relationships than that? Of course he was bloody good at them. He probably met different girls every night, a lot prettier and more engaging than she was. Flirting his way into a one night stand with her was probably all in a day's work for him.

Best case scenario, which she absolutely was not going to let herself think about, meant assuming that Owen wasn't upstairs right now deciding how best to backtrack out of what had happened between them. Assuming he really did like her beyond what had happened the night before, she knew exactly how this thing would proceed. She knew from experience. Her mother's and her own. Things might tick along for a while, looking like they were all going well. There would be nothing discernible that was wrong with the relationship, but underneath it all there would be plenty. And if she let herself go down that path then at some point would come the moment at which a lens was put in front of the situation that suddenly made everything clear. All would not be hunky-dory. Something or someone would come along that was a better bet than Amy Wilson.

It always did.

Fortunately, because she had a handle on how life worked for Amy Wilson, she had the perfect action plan already in place. Hadn't she spent the last couple of years operating very successfully on that premise? There was no room for emotion in the running of her life. Excluding emotion and using her mind without reference to her heart meant *efficiency*. It meant excluding poor judgement. It worked like a dream in her working life and it did a pretty damn good job in her private life too.

She stood near the entrance to the beautifully dressed dining room, with its perfect white table linen and silver cutlery. Ostensibly she was on hand in case the bride or groom should need to ask anything about the day ahead, but actually she was waiting on tenterhooks to see if Luke would drag himself down here, and if he did how hung over he might be.

The delicious smell of fresh coffee and smoked bacon drifted across the room. Classical music played in the background, something light and soothing to ease the guests into the day. None of it removed the feeling of nervous twirly butterflies in her stomach and as if that wasn't enough to cope with, her heart launched into insane skittering as Owen appeared in the doorway. As she watched he paused to smooth a hand through his shower-damp hair and turned the movement into a nonchalant shrug as he noticed her eyes on him. He sauntered over to her.

'Got back to your room without being sacked then?' he drawled, a cheeky smile spreading across his handsome face that made a wave of heat curl through her stomach and end up somewhere near her toes. Her heart clattered against her ribcage and she clasped her hands together in front of her to stop them shaking. She widened incredulous eyes at him and glanced around to see if any of the dining room staff had heard.

'Breakfast is a mixture of self-service and table service,' she said loudly, tripping out the standard spiel. She waved a hand toward the breakfast buffet. 'There's a selection of cereal, yogurt and fresh fruit. Breakfast rolls and meats if you'd prefer something a little more continental. Or if you'd like a full cooked breakfast please just take a seat at one of the tables and one of the waitresses will be along shortly to take your order and organise coffee or tea.'

There was a long pause during which she waved a few more people past and tried to ignore the roll of his eyes.

'There's plenty of tables,' she pointed out when he made no move.

'You mean you really *are* just going to write last night off as if it never happened?' he hissed in a stage whisper.

She nodded, smiling past him at a couple of guests as they entered the room.

'Of course. What did you think I was going to do?' The restaurant manager was looking at them with interest and she spoke through her beaming teeth. 'If you could please try and be a bit

59

discreet it would be helpful. Last night was just…one of those things.'

'One of those things,' he repeated.

'No need to make it more than it was.'

She felt rather than saw an almost imperceptible stiffening of his shoulders. Then it disappeared as he leaned in towards her.

'No problem,' he said.

An ill-judged jolt of regret kicked her in the stomach as he simply turned and headed toward a vacant table and took a seat. She gritted her teeth firmly against it. There was no room for regret in this scenario, or any other feeling about the situation, not if she wanted to get this job. Tomorrow Owen Lloyd would be checking out of the hotel and getting back to his normal life. And she would still be Amy Wilson, who'd worked her butt off and waited in the wings for an opportunity this good ever since she'd left college. No way was she throwing this job away because of a stupid blip. No matter how deliriously gorgeous it might have been.

Still her traitorous eyes kept sliding across to Owen until the sound of loud voices in the lobby diverted her attention. Two minutes later and Luke sauntered into the dining room in a scruffy jeans-and-t-shirt combo. He drew to a halt in front of her and gave her a salute. For heaven's sake, he still looked half-cut. Then again, it was hard to tell with his mussed-up appearance.

'Feeling OK, are you?' she said.

He gave her a wink.

'Great thanks. Full steam ahead for the champagne breakfast.'

'I'm surprised you feel like drinking ever again,' she said.

He patted her shoulder as he passed.

'Every night is party night, babe,' he said. 'Don't knock it.'

She watched as he took a seat at a table with a group of his mates and loudly ordered a full English. He might be here to get married but from all she'd seen he was still clearly living the life of a bachelor. She hoped Sabrina knew what she was letting herself in for.

Conrad was up and running with the reworked drinks plan. For some reason it gave her no sense of satisfaction to tick another thing off her to-do list. In fact the usual buzz she felt when a wedding was in full swing seemed to be missing today. She felt oddly deflated, as if she was just going through the motions and her job satisfaction had been sucked out of her.

'You *slept* with him?' he said, virtually as soon as she walked through the door. Mercifully the bar was empty at this time of day except for the occasional appearance of Lavington staff.

Her stomach lurched guiltily.

'I didn't say that.' Bloody hell did he have some psychic ability?

'You didn't have to.' He grinned. 'It's written all over your face.'

'So you're going to mix Peach Bellinis as the celebratory post-ceremony drink then?' she said loudly over Conrad as one of the duty managers walked past the door and glanced in. She lowered her voice to an urgent hiss, 'Do you think you could keep your voice down? The management have ears everywhere. If word of this gets out it'll be instant dismissal.'

'You should have thought of that before.'

'I *did* think of that before. It just kind of went out of my head. It was late. I'd had a crappy day. I felt like the most unattractive, dull person on the planet. Luke Pemberton is right in the middle of the test wedding for my new job and he's walking evidence that I really am the last tomato in the shop. That squishy one that looks OK at first but that bursts over everyone's hands and gets put back when they get a closer look.'

Conrad pursed his lips in a moue of distaste.

'Please! Do you need to be so graphic? Stop with the horrible food analogies.'

She grinned.

'Sorry. I'm just trying to explain. Owen is just so great to talk to, not to mention an incredible flirt. Maybe I wanted to be with someone, just for once, where I didn't come off feeling like the understudy.' She sighed. 'We kind of got into this mutual moment where we agreed we could do whatever we wanted and there'd be no comeback.'

Conrad fanned himself with a drinks mat.

'That sounds extremely hot, darling.'

'It was.'

So hot, her insides felt squidgy whenever she thought of it. In that moment, she really had been the real deal. That's how he'd made her feel.

'And is there?'

'What?'

'No comeback?'

She stared behind him at the glossy backlit bar, wishing she could answer with a resounding and truthful no.

'I'll have to let you know on that one. Right now I've got a wedding to run.'

Flowers…check. Beautiful arrangements of dusky pink and cream roses filled the ballroom. Registrar…check. String quartet playing a delightful range of background music…check. Chairs with their white linen covers and dusky pink bows slowly filling with wedding guests…check. Best man and bridegroom…

Amy glanced at the front row of chairs on the right hand side of the aisle, where if this day was going to plan Luke should now be sitting, ideally dressed in something a bit less rock-god than he'd worn thus far. Owen should be next to him with the rings in the pocket of a co-ordinating suit.

Best man and bridegroom?

The front row was empty.

She was good. She wasn't about to panic.

She took a step back into the small bar adjacent to the ballroom, where guests could buy drinks and mingle prior to the ceremony and swept her eyes quickly around the room. No sign of either Luke or Owen. She checked her wristwatch. Only twenty minutes before Sabrina and her entourage of glossy attendants would be sweeping into the ballroom. Luke should have been here for at least the past hour, welcoming guests and getting ready for his bride.

She was calm. Punctuality wasn't Luke's strong point. And Owen was probably on the phone to one of his string of bars. Excuses, excuses…

Crossing the marble floored lobby at a moderate walking pace that screamed total control, she picked up one of the phones on the Reception desk and punched in the number of Luke's room. It rang and rang. And only then did a hideous possibility cross her mind for the first time. Yes, she was the self-styled queen of wedding management, and she'd ironed out many a last-minute organisational problem in her time, but she'd never had a groom stand up a bride before. Not on her watch. Her stomach gave an unexpected nervous lurch.

Her mind sideslipped unexpectedly into an image of her small self in her pink meringue of a bridesmaid dress with flowers in her hair, trying to understand why her mother was crying her eyes out on what had been touted as the best day of their lives. The day when their little family-unit-in-waiting would become a reality. The day when her stand-in father, Roger, would become her proper dad. The image took her breath away and she pressed a hand to her chest and forced her mind to take focus.

She headed for the stairs, picking up speed, and nearly collided with Owen on his way down them two at a time. He was dressed in the same grey morning suit as the ushers, a dusky pink hand-kerchief in the jacket pocket, the neck of his crisp white shirt open and a dusky pink rose spray in his lapel. His dark hair was slightly tousled and he looked jaw-droppingly gorgeous, as if he'd just stepped from the pages of a glossy wedding magazine. He screeched to a halt in front of her.

Any flutter of attraction she might have felt at seeing him was completely squashed by the gravity of the situation.

'What the hell is going on?' she said. '*Where* is Luke? Half of London's hip and trendy are waiting for him in the ballroom and

Sabrina will be pitching up any second.'

'You might want to sit down,' he said.

CHAPTER 8

'He says he can't go through with it,' Owen said as she followed him up the stairs in disbelief. 'I was just on my way to find you, I thought maybe you could get through to him since you know each other.'

She stormed down the corridor behind Owen, the truth of the situation really grabbing her now, the implications growing and multiplying, filling her mind. The logistical nightmare of standing down the staff, of informing the guests that the wedding wouldn't be going ahead, of consoling an inconsolable bride, all of it paraded through her head like a bad dream. Instead of just rubber stamping her new permanent job contract, her every move this weekend would instead be scrutinised by the management. She'd wanted this wedding to be absolute perfection – a showcase for her talent, and now the whole thing was unravelling. All these thoughts slapped into her brain full force as she strode into Owen's hotel room. Luke was sitting on the sofa in his wedding suit with his fashionably dishevelled head in his hands. Clothes littered the room and there was an eye watering smell of expensive aftershave.

'What the bloody hell are you doing?' she shouted, an unexpected surge of frustrated anger at the situation rising aggressively through her from nowhere, driving out her normal poised professionalism. 'Sabrina will be walking up the aisle any minute and this wedding has to go smoothly, without a hitch. You can't just drop out because you've got cold feet. What kind of monster are you? Get that jacket on, butch up and get down those stairs.'

He held up both hands in submission as she clapped them to her hips.

'You can shout all you want, Amy. I can't marry Sabrina now. Things have changed. It wouldn't be fair. And I know your job is the be all and end all but I can't get married just so you look good in front of your boss.'

Cold rage welled up from a place so deep she hadn't known it had existed. All the old feelings of rejection and bitterness and broken hope. The unfairness of her mother's shame and embarrassment and no one to shout at or ask for an explanation because Roger had simply disappeared with nothing more than a vague note of apology. The resentment rose up and Luke recoiled in amazement as she yelled at him.

'It's not about my job you idiot! Oh bloody hell! You *cannot* do this to her, do you understand me? You will *break* her.' Her voice cracked with the force of it.

'Let's just all calm down, shall we?' Owen said.

The surprise in his tone cut through her fury and she glanced sideways at him, seeing his raised eyebrows and *lighten-up* expression. She shook her head lightly as if to clear it, realising she might have gone a bit far. Her throat felt vaguely peppery where she'd raised her voice to rasping point.

'I *am* calm,' she snapped, lowering her voice and demonstrating the fact by sitting down on one of the chairs. She took some deep breaths, bewildered by her own depth of feeling about this. This was *not* her mother's wedding. She had no personal stake in this. And Luke Pemberton, for all his shallow faults, was not Roger Corbett of twenty odd years ago.

That didn't detract from the fact that his behaviour was outrageous. Her mind slipped back to the end of her own relationship with Luke, such as it had been. To his insistence that it hadn't been serious.

'I don't know why I'm actually surprised,' she said to Owen, exasperated. 'He's obviously a commitment phobic. He made it clear when we broke up that he was a free spirit who could never be tied down, when there I was thinking we could run and run and eventually get settled. My bad. I accept that. I chucked myself into work and let it confirm what I already knew – marriage in all its forms is a total waste of time. I thought he was living the free spirit dream when he legged it to London and never bothered keeping in touch. I couldn't have been more gobsmacked when he turned up and told me freedom was all a load of bollocks and he was getting spliced.' She shrugged. 'This is just Luke reverting to type and to hell with the consequences.'

'I am NOT a commitment phobic,' Luke said. 'Will you quit talking like I'm not here? You and I had a laugh Amy. It was never going to last. It was nothing personal. Commitment just never came into it. With Sabrina it's different. I want more than anything to be married to her.'

The usual spike of inferiority rose in her stomach and she squashed it back down. She had absolutely no interest in Luke, she wanted nothing more than for him to get downstairs and get married to Sabrina. But there was still that sharp reminder that Amy wasn't the kind of person who could attract that kind of lifelong love and security.

'Well now's your chance!' she said. 'Get downstairs! She'll be the one in the white frock with a bouquet.'

'I can't,' he said. His voice sounded strangled. 'My recording contract's fallen through. Finance problems with the record company. All new acquisitions are on hold. I haven't even recorded anything yet. I only found out this morning.' His head slumped back into his hands. 'Sabrina won't want me now.'

'Mate, that sucks.' Owen pressed a hand on Luke's shoulder. 'Have you got legal advice?'

Luke shook his head. 'I've only just heard from my management company. I haven't even thought what to do yet. I've spent so much money on the back of the signing…'

'None of this actually means that Sabrina would want to pull out,' Amy said. 'Don't you think she'd want to stand by you if you're having problems?'

'I can't expect her to. Not now.'

His blanket assumption that he was somehow doing Sabrina a favour here brought a new surge of frustration. Amy leaned in towards him.

'Listen to me, Luke. I know what I'm talking about.'

'You don't believe in marriage. Despite the insane irony of your career choice,' he pointed out irritably. 'So how can you possibly know what I'm talking about?'

She glanced at Owen. He was watching her intently.

'Because I've been there,' she said simply.

They were staring at her. She took a deep breath.

'My mother was a single parent,' she said. 'Up until I was five years old. Then she met this amazing man. Good job, great attitude, wasn't put off by the fact she had a kid. I don't remember her ever being that happy, even now. Two years he was with us, just dating her for the first months, and then after a while he moved in. Everything was good. I knew it was, because they decided to get married.' She looked down at her hands, remembering. 'Everything was booked. The registry office, the town hall. Invitations went out. Sandwiches were made. There were flowers. Mum and I had beautiful outfits.' She paused. 'And he didn't turn up.'

'You mean…' Owen said.

She nodded.

'He stood her up. Stood *us* up. And he didn't just not turn up that day. When we eventually got home, he'd packed his stuff and gone. She never had a word from him beyond a note he'd left that said it was for the best.' She pressed her lips tightly together. 'It's never for the best, though. Not when you do it like that. My mother was devastated.'

So was I, her mind added.

She looked at Luke.

'I'm sorry for going off like that at you,' she said. 'I wasn't really aiming it at you. I was just so frustrated because you might think you're doing Sabrina a favour by backing out but you couldn't be more wrong. You need to give her an explanation and let *her* have that choice.'

A long pause and then Luke spoke.

'Where is she?'

Sweet relief flooded in. Amy stood up, hoping that Sabrina had heard of the concept of fashionable lateness.

'She's in the honeymoon suite. I'll go ahead and get everyone else out and the two of you can talk.'

'Are you fucking kidding me? Don't you know it's bad luck to see the bride before the wedding?' Sabrina's incredulous voice was muffled but perfectly audible through the bathroom door of the honeymoon suite.

'Angel, that's just some old wives claptrap.' Luke spoke soothingly, his mouth inches away from the keyhole. 'We need to talk. This is serious. Please, just open up.'

Amy took a deep breath, closed the honeymoon suite door discreetly behind her and smiled her way soothingly through Sabrina's entourage of bridesmaids. They stood bemused and squashed in a mass of pink and white tulle and satin in the ten-foot-wide corridor, where Amy had managed to usher them under enormous protest so that Luke and Sabrina could have a few minutes alone.

Downstairs, she stood at the front of the ballroom and announced to the bemused guests that there'd been a slight delay in the proceedings but that everything was under control, a round of drinks would be available in the bar and the ceremony would begin in half an hour.

'Let's hope half an hour's long enough,' she said to Owen as the guests began to file back into the bar and the string quartet launched back into their pre-wedding repertoire. 'I'm heading out for five minutes before it all kicks off again. I need some air.'

She found herself hoping that Sabrina wasn't with Luke for the kudos and wanted to marry him no matter what. She checked herself. This was getting a bit too close to happy ever after to sit well with her long ingrained cynicism.

'Want some company?'

Her heart turned over softly. The day had spiralled into a nightmare but he'd been right there next to her, trying to help sort things out. A wistful pang slipped through her. She liked him. It wasn't just about the sex. They understood each other. It would be so lovely to believe that this feeling could last but she knew better than that. She would be a fool to think this could possibly exist past this weekend. The whole reason it had been so perfect between them was the momentariness of it.

He walked out through the lobby with her. Regular hotel guests went about their business, checking in, taking coffee at the cosy groupings of sofas. She pushed a path through the revolving doors, conscious for that brief moment of his closeness before they were both ejected onto the sunny pavement. She took a left turn and walked slowly, loath to stray too far from the front door in case some other crisis kicked in.

'What the hell made you want to work in weddings?' Owen asked, strolling next to her. His hands were deep in his pockets and he was looking down at the pavement thoughtfully. 'I mean, after what happened with your mother I could understand it if you never wanted to even think about weddings again, let alone organise them for a living. It all makes sense now, all that stuff about not believing in happy ever after. It must have been the most awful day. I saw those little nieces of Sabrina's in there, in their dresses with their hair all done up. Isn't all that stuff meant to be a dream for a little girl?'

She paused and leaned back against the smooth cream brick of the hotel wall, letting the afternoon bustle of the street pass them by. The sun was deliciously warm on her face.

'It was. My dress was this pink thing. Covered in frills with a big satin sash. I remember I had my hair curled. I'd never had that done before and I was so excited.' She glanced at him. He leaned on one shoulder against the wall, his expression sympathetic. 'It wasn't really about the day though. I don't think it would have made any difference if it was the most expensive, rich wedding in the universe. It was what it was going to mean that counted.'

'Your parents getting married.'

'Roger wasn't my real father.' She pressed her lips together. 'I've never met my real father, he left before I was born. I hated Roger at first but when I got used to sharing her with him I thought he was the best thing since sliced bread. Finally I was going to be like all my friends and have a proper mum and dad. Be part of a proper family.' She swallowed. 'I know it was years ago and all in the past but sometimes I still feel sorry for that little girl in the pink dress.'

He reached out and took her hand in his, threading his fingers through hers. It was nice. It didn't have to mean the world. It was just nice that he wanted to make her feel better.

'I wish I could have told Roger what he'd done to us by just making that autocratic decision not to give it a go. By disappearing without leaving a reason. You find yourself reading all kinds of things into it – if I'd behaved better might he have stayed, that kind of thing. That's why I may have gone a bit overboard back there with Luke.'

'You think?'

His smile was gentle. She met it with a small one of her own.

'It's like part of me got stuck in that corridor outside the registry office. My mum's best friend was there in an awful purple frock. And there were people from her work. Our neighbours. I can remember what the carpet looked like, this hardwearing stuff with a paisley print like an old people's home. I remember it so

71

clearly. When I came to the Lavington I couldn't believe how stunning the wedding facilities are. Like a palace.' She shrugged. 'The registry office would have done. If he'd just gone through with it. My mother's never really gotten over it. She's never let another man into her life since.'

She suddenly realised all this talk of weddings from the past on the back of her outburst at Luke might not be presenting her as the most grounded person he'd ever met.

'I know how it looks,' she said. 'Like I'm some crazy Miss Havisham person who's wedding-obsessed because of the day I never had, but it really isn't like that. I started out just working on a local hotel reception, then I moved into an assistant events manager role, handling all sorts of parties and corporate meetings. Then it started to get popular to have a full-on wedding event rather than a church ceremony followed by a reception. Hotels were given wedding licences. Weddings were – are - big business. It was a natural career progression that I ended up handling more and more of them.' She paused, then admitted, 'Maybe there is a bit of a dark fascination with all the girly stuff you get these days. The flowers, the dresses, the wedding favours. But only because I see it all as window dressing. The underlying sentiment is the important thing and I don't think marriage is a condition of whether that's there or not. Maybe Luke and Sabrina will have it. Maybe they won't. My job is to basically throw them a massive party and I don't read anything more into it than that.'

As Owen walked back to the hotel next to her he realised that he'd had a fifteen minute window right there when he could have ducked out to call around his bar managers. Saturday: busiest night of the week and he was strolling in the sunshine.

The bars hadn't entered his mind for a second. He'd taken a walk with her because he wanted to make sure she was OK. Amy with her cold and focused work ethic. It must have taken a lot for her to talk openly like that about her stepfather. It certainly went some way to explaining her emotionless approach towards weddings. He felt an irrational surge of anger toward this Roger, who he'd never met, but who had stamped on her dreams when she was just a little kid.

What the hell was happening to him? Like he had time to get involved in other people's problems.

The sooner Luke got this wedding back on track the better.

CHAPTER 9

The calm after the storm. Amy stood unobtrusively next to a plinth on which an enormous flower arrangement stood and watched the party from the sidelines.

This was the part of a wedding that she liked the most. The ceremony out of the way, the wedding breakfast served without a hitch. Speeches done and dusted and evening entertainment perfectly pulled-off. Luke and Sabrina swayed together on the softly-lit dancefloor, so closely entwined that if it weren't for the ivory of her dress you wouldn't be able to see where one person started and the other one ended.

It had all worked out well for Luke in the end. Despite his cold feet it seemed Sabrina wanted him for who he was after all, and not for the recording contract. A wistful pang twisted at her chest. Perhaps if Roger had given her mother a proper chance their lives might have turned out differently.

Her eyes had strayed again and again to Owen as the day had progressed. He'd played the best man role to perfection, charming everyone. His speech had been off-the-cuff and funny without the slightest mention of anyone's cold feet, finishing with a toast to the bride and groom that was met with cheers. Now he was at the bar talking animatedly to Conrad, who was smiling through gritted teeth, undoubtedly offering advice on what drinks he should be serving.

He'd barely spoken to her all day. She squashed the seeds of disappointment before they could start to grow. Why should he want to make time to chat to her? His best man role was his priority and quite right too. And she should be steering well clear of him. The weekend was almost sewn up and the last thing she needed now was to shoot herself in the promotional foot by perpetuating things with him.

Even from here she could see Conrad's look of relief and exasperated roll of the eyes as Owen left him to it at the bar. Amusement disappeared into a surge of stomach flutters as he headed her way across the dancefloor, a glass in his hand containing blush pink liquid and a cocktail stick.

'Try this,' he said, coming to a halt next to her and holding it out.

Alarm bells screamed in her head. *Over-familiarity with one of the guests. Drinking on duty. Inappropriate behaviour.* She took the glass anyway and took a sip.

'Strawberries with a kick,' she managed, trying not to gasp as it burned its way into her stomach. Its strength was hidden by the delicious fruit crush. 'Very nice.' She handed it back to him.

He nodded across the room at Luke and Sabrina, now sitting close together at one of the candlelit tables, talking quietly.

'It all worked out great in the end,' he said.

'I know.' She followed his gaze. 'My work is almost done. I'm here overnight again, but in reality I won't be needed. The restaurant staff will manage breakfast and then everyone checks out. All in all, it's been a success.'

'You see, it's not all doom and gloom.'

'I never said it was,' she said. 'Nothing would make me happier than for Luke and Sabrina to live happily ever after. I just prefer not to rely on another person for my own happiness, that's all.'

'Of course. Your work-hard-and-no-time-for-play rule,' he said. He took a sip of the pink cocktail himself. 'You know it basically means you have no life. You can't let what happened to your mum affect you like that.'

'It isn't just about that,' she said. 'I mean it might have affected my attitude towards weddings and marriage, but it's more that it was the beginning of a recurring theme in my life.'

'What do you mean?'

She watched as two of Sabrina's little bridesmaids twirled their way around the middle of the dancefloor.

'Roger – my stepfather – just couldn't go through with it. That's what he said in the note he left for us. It was the lifelong commitment of it that was the sticking point for him. He could go with it while there were no deadlines. For some reason making it official made him feel hemmed in and he couldn't cope. The *responsibility* of it, he said. But that's just an excuse. If he loved us he would have been there. When you pare it right down we were ok for now but he didn't want to put a ring on it.'

She squeezed her hands together, trying to get it across to him so he'd understand instead of thinking she was some basket-case loner.

'OK-for-now has been a bit of a pattern for me ever since,' she said. 'I was always the mediocre achiever at school, no matter how hard I tried. Then I spent years in the hotel industry never quite landing the managerial role. I applied so many times but until now I was forever the assistant doing the donkey work without the credit.' She counted things off on her fingers. 'Same with relationships. They've never worked for me, never lasted. Take Luke for example, we dated, it all seemed to go well enough, and then he got a job offer and bailed. You heard him in the hotel room this afternoon – he never saw our relationship as anything more than casual. I'd read it totally wrong. He said he never wanted to be tied down, but in reality he didn't want to be tied down by *me*. Neither did Roger.' She smoothed her jacket. 'I decided when I moved to London that since there was no point relying on anyone else for my security or happiness, I'd make my own. No more investing in other people only for them to let me down.

I'd keep my emotions and my actions totally separate, no getting involved. And so far, that's working for me.'

'Maybe you just haven't met the right person,' he said. 'You never know what the future might hold.'

His concerned expression made her steel herself. She didn't want his sympathy or concern. She'd said too much and now he probably saw her as some underachieving saddo.

'Yes I do,' she said. 'If I work hard it will hold a home of my own. That's my big plan. I don't need the right person for that, I can get it for myself. And anyway, all this proclaiming that I will meet Mr Right one day and that I shouldn't write off marriage,' she touched his chest with a fingertip. 'You're hardly the poster boy for that, are you? You think family ties are something that hold you back, don't you?'

That comment was so astute that Owen had to take a moment, take a sip of his drink to collect his thoughts.

'Not especially.'

He shoved his parents' most recent email out of his mind, as yet unanswered. The resentment remained, like a stubborn stain that was impossible to completely wash away. When he'd been trying to get his idea off the ground there had been no interest or enthusiasm, only attempts to talk him out of it. They'd made it clear they wouldn't be prepared to put any money toward his 'little adventure', as they saw it. Not that he'd ever asked them for a penny. But he'd made it now. He was a success, and now they wanted to fix things, now they were keen to build bridges and pull him back into the family fold. Now that he'd done good. If the bar had failed they'd still be giving him the cold shoulder.

'Please! Every move you make is with a nod towards work. I mean look at you this evening – advising my perfectly capable diva of a Bar Manager on what drinks he should be serving. Slipping behind the bar on Luke's stag night. Planning your invasion of Europe in every spare moment. I saw the pictures of bar premises in your hotel room. So tell me – when did YOU last go out on a proper date? And I'm not counting flirting with women in your cocktail bar.'

He raised a hand without thinking and pushed it uncomfortably through his hair.

She was right about the flirting. It went with the job. Working a bar meant chatting to the single girls, mixing drinks, being the life and soul of every party. It rarely progressed beyond the flirt stage, however. Now he thought about it, until this weekend he hadn't been to bed with anyone in months. His goal, the success of his business, was his absolute focus.

'I don't really date,' he said. 'It's such a time suck.'

She nodded triumphantly.

'You see. You're worse than me,' she said.

When he didn't answer she looked at him questioningly.

'I do get the point,' she said. 'At first you had something to prove with your family because you'd chosen not to take over the farm. But you've got a chain of bars now. You're a big success. You've shown your family it wasn't just a pipe dream. So what happens now, do you just carry on and on, building the Lloyd cocktail empire until it's world dominating? Where does it all end?' She pointed an emphatic finger at his chest and smiled her cute smile up at his face, making his heart turn over in spite of himself. 'I hate to break it to you, but basically *you* have no life either.'

He burst out laughing.

'We're as bad as each other. You're right.' The moment swept him along. 'So you want to have no life together?' he said.

Her eyes met and held his. His pulse was thundering.

'We're both here until tomorrow, you must be just about to clock off and my job here is done. What do you say?'

The vagueness of the proposal made it somehow so appealing, knowing exactly where she stood made it safe. He'd be checking out in the morning. She'd be back to work as usual. No one would miss her now her shift was over. Why shouldn't she have one more perfect night where she knew she was the priority? It was only when it started to mean something that things started to go wrong.

'I'm in the staff quarters tonight again,' she said, as if that closed the subject.

'I'll walk you back,' he said.

When she didn't object he put the half-finished strawberry cocktail down on the nearest table. What few guests they saw as they crossed the lobby were having far too good a time to notice them.

'The staff quarters are down there,' she said, stopping at a corridor that led to the back of the hotel. 'You can't come back there, so I should really say goodnight here.'

His gaze found hers and held it, the question hanging between them in the tense silence. Then he reached across, took her hand in his and tugged her instead toward the lift.

As the lift doors slid closed, shutting out the deserted lobby, he pushed her against the velvet wall and slid both hands into her hair. The lift jolted softly into life beneath her feet as he took her lower lip between his own and kissed her, his tongue caressing gently. Her arms crept up to lock behind his neck, her fingers sliding through his dark hair as the contours of his body fit perfectly against hers.

A harder jolt as the lift came to a stop and Owen had the presence of mind to take a backward pace out of her personal space, leaving her breathing in quick soft gasps. Left to her own mind set, meltingly focused on his touch, she would have had no care if the doors had slid open to reveal half the staff in the hotel.

The corridor was empty. He took her by the hand.

His room again but this time there was no sense of urgency or rush. The desire was as strong as ever but now he took his time, savouring every moment. Fast heat was replaced by slow lingering caresses. He lifted her into his arms and carried her across the room to lay her gently on the bed. As he undressed her he lingered over each new bit of exposed skin, kissing and stroking her until she was naked and writhing with desire. Then she lay in the soft glow of the table lamp, too aroused to feel inhibited as he shed his own clothes, meeting her gaze steadily until his wedding suit was cast aside on the floor and he joined her on the bed.

Turning her gently on her side, the hard muscular contours of his chest pressed against her back as soft kisses teased at the nape of her neck and his hands slipped around her, one cupping her breasts, the other sliding lower, down the flat of her stomach, lower still, until he teased his way inside her with his fingers, making her gasp softly. He used his legs to turn with her until she was on her stomach, and eased her thighs gently apart, then his fingers were replaced by his rock hard erection as he smoothly thrust inside her to the hilt.

She turned her head in ecstasy, the sheet cool against her hot cheek as he took her with a slow and delicious rhythm, his fingers sliding beneath her to tease her most sensitive nub as he filled her again and again. Her climax began to linger within reach and he took her to the brink of it before slowing his pace, then climbing again, until she begged him to finish it and he raised himself on his palms and thrust hard and fast. As she cried out her pleasure he gasped his own against her shoulder.

The room was quiet. She lay against him in a tangle of bedsheets and pillows, listening to his breathing evening out. His hands, curled tightly around her, slowly relaxed into a gentle caressing stroke of her neck and hair.

We're both here until tomorrow.

She forced her mind to replay that remark of his over and over again because what just happened hadn't felt like a moment of madness or a quick shag to her. It had felt like he cared about her. It had felt loving.

She was imagining it. Obviously. Because he'd made it clear he wasn't thinking beyond the morning.

The very reason she'd gone with this was because he so clearly didn't want to make anything of it. She wasn't about to hope for or expect more than that. To do so would be to set herself up for the most predictable fall yet. From the back of her mind she grabbed the three no's - *no emotion, no personal involvement, no distraction* – and applied them like mad.

'This doesn't mean anything after tonight, right?' she said. 'Back to real life tomorrow.'

She lay against his chest, her hair lying silkily against his neck. He picked up a strand of it, tested its softness against his fingertips.

It might just as well have been him saying that. They were so alike. It was the same point he'd made with the few girls he'd been with these last years, making sure they always knew it was just fun, careful to emphasise it was nothing heavy. He should be feeling fantastic – a weekend of celebration with sex thrown in, that's what this was, and how great to share it with someone who felt the same, no need to spell out all the caveats for once. And yet for some insane unfathomable reason he wanted more than that this time. Perhaps that was the reason right there - because he knew he couldn't have it. Human nature, that was all.

That explanation felt uncomfortable. All he knew was that the idea of checking out tomorrow and never seeing her again made him feel bloody miserable. For once he'd met someone with the same outlook as him, and in her it seemed such a waste. And it brought with it a needling unease as to what that said about his own life. He'd spent so long setting himself free from family ties and guilt and responsibility to others that avoiding any new close relationship had become a habit. He groped for a way of seeing her again that didn't feel like it could end up being a distraction from all that he'd worked for, so important to him after all he'd given up to pursue it.

When he didn't answer, she pulled herself up onto one elbow and looked at him. Her brown eyes were soft and a smile touched the corner of her lips. He reached up to slide his thumb along her cheekbone, wanting to feel the softness of her skin.

'What are you doing next Thursday?' he said, before he could think it over and put a hold on his tongue.

A tiny frown line appeared between her eyebrows. There was a look of wary hope in her eyes now, as if there was a fifty-fifty chance she might stay put or bolt from the bed at any moment.

'Working,' she said, carefully.

Had he really expected anything else? She wasn't exactly exuding enthusiasm but he shoved on ahead regardless. The idea was out there now, there was no rewinding time.

'Me too,' he said. 'How about we do something really crazy and just go out after work. Have a late dinner maybe. What do you say?'

The smile didn't reappear. Not a good sign. His heart was doing cartwheels in his chest. What was wrong with him? Why the hell did this feel like such a big deal?

'This has been a laugh, right?' he said, trying again. 'There's no need for this to be an end to it, just because the weekend happens to be over. It doesn't need to be full-on. We've both got work commitments, I know that, but when we're both free…when we've got time. What do you think?'

'Don't make it into something it's not,' she said.

'I'm not,' he said. Then immediately backtracked, an unexpected burst of indignance rising through him at the instant dismissal. 'How do you know it's not anything? It could be something if you gave it half a chance.'

Disappointment curled through her but she forced a smile.

'Fitting us in around *work* doesn't equate to it being something, Owen,' she said. 'So it's OK for us to date as long as it comes second to work. No interfering with that – right? You don't want to get too close in case I get in the way or hold you back.'

Now she sat up and swung her legs out of the bed, her shoulder hiding her face as she reached for her clothes. He sat up too, pushing both hands into his hair as he stared up at the ceiling in frustration.

'I thought you'd jump at this with your emotion-free love life philosophy,' he said.

'I went with *this weekend* because of my emotion-free love life philosophy. I went with *tonight* for that reason.' She shook her head. 'It won't work, Owen. Not any longer than this.'

He shook his head in confusion.

'I thought this was what you wanted. You told me you were work-obsessed, ambitious, that you don't need to rely on anyone else because you've got your own security covered. You don't do happy-ever-afters and that's fin. I get that. What I'm suggesting is happy-for-now.'

The fact that she'd expected it didn't make it any easier. You'd think after all this time the same old let-down would lose its bite.

'Maybe happy-for-now is all I'm good for, Owen.' She shrugged. 'But it doesn't mean it's all I want. If you'd said *Amy, I really like you and I'd like to make a go of this, get to know you better* – maybe I might have made a leap of faith for that. It would have been scary but it might have been worth it. What I want you to say is sod the emotional claptrap. Sod work. Sod everything. Let's see each other again because I like you, not *let's perpetuate this thing because it fits well with work.* I've been here before and I'm not being your bloody *filler*, great for you right now because you're work obsessed but easy to leave behind when things change. You're completely defined by your business, Owen. You are *Loco.* And deep down, I don't think you have room for anything else in your life.'

She was shaking her head, not looking at him. Clothes pulled together now, she began to dress, jabbing buttons into buttonholes as if she couldn't escape fast enough.

'You're leaving? You don't need to go now. It's the middle of the night.'

'I need to get some sleep, I've got a meeting tomorrow with the recruitment team, a debrief of the wedding and I need to make a good impression.' She glanced at her wristwatch. 'It's not midnight yet, you can still get back to the party.'

As if she thought this had been some waste of an evening and he would have preferred to be downstairs in the bar? His head spun with the sudden change in her and with exasperation at how impossible she was to read. He wasn't sure what bothered him more – the fact she was just walking away or the way it made him feel.

She was dressed now, stepping into her shoes, crossing the room towards the door. He sat forward in the bed, the covers rucked around his waist.

'I'm not interested in going back to the party,' he said. 'What's the rush? You don't even want to think about it? Bloody hell am I that hideous an option?'

Hand on the door handle, she tipped her head back and sighed briefly up at the ceiling before she looked back.

'You're not a hideous option.' She shook her head slowly at him, an apologetic smile on her pretty face. 'I'm just not up for this. Not on those terms. I know they might be the best terms I'll ever get, but I've been the warm-up act too many times to want to do it all again now. Even for someone as gorgeous as you. How long would it last before something better came along? Weeks? Months? I don't know the answer to any of those questions but I do know there *will* be a time frame because there always is with me.' She tugged the door open. 'I hope Europe works out well for you. Goodbye Owen.'

She pressed her lips together as she walked down the hallway. There were no staff around to see her, no guests in sight as she took the back stairs and headed for the staff quarters. She'd made the right decision. She knew that with all her rational mind. Sharp and clean, this was the best way to go. Kill off all feelings before they could grow, while she still had control of them. She changed into her old checked pyjamas and climbed into the hideous bed.

Sleep had been unbelievably elusive based on how tired she was. Owen stayed on her mind no matter how hard she tried to count sheep or think of other things. She could close her eyes and still feel his touch.

By morning doubts had crept in.

Maybe she had dismissed him too hastily last night. She hadn't exactly given him the chance for discussion, after all. She'd simply heard what he said about work and had immediately pegged herself as his second priority, but hadn't she been just as rabid about her own career plans as he was? Hadn't their whole connection been based on their mutual aim to work themselves into the ground? She thought back to his flirt on that first evening, bloody hell it felt like years ago – could it really have only been two days?

'Have a drink with me. We can toast independent workaholism.'

Was he so wrong to assume that maybe *she* might not want a relationship that interfered with her career?

There was still breakfast before the wedding guests checked out. Another chance to talk things through instead of just letting things lie.

She showered, dressed in her uniform and did the best she could to hide the dark shadows under her eyes with makeup. Her head ached as she headed down to the restaurant where the air was filled with the aroma of hot coffee and fresh pastries. Her stomach was a mass of fluttering. Only one or two guests so far, neither of them Owen. She hovered near the entrance to the dining room for the best part of an hour, her heart sinking a little more with each minute that passed, before she thought to check at reception.

Owen Lloyd had checked out at six-thirty while she was still in her room. Way before breakfast even began.

'Had to get back to work, he said,' the receptionist told her. 'Some kind of bar job, busy at weekends.'

She walked away from the reception desk feeling utterly empty and absolutely tired out.

What had she expected – that he might ask her out again over his full English, when she'd already knocked him back once? He *had to get back to work* – what other information did she need about his priorities? She'd called it right after all, she would never have come first with someone like that.

She wished someone would tell that to her stomach, now a sick churning mass of disappointment.

85

Luke and Sabrina came to say goodbye.

'I'll make sure the final balance on the weekend is paid off within the next week,' Luke said, when Sabrina had kissed her on the cheek and moved away. 'I just need a day or two to get things back on track.'

'It's fine,' she said. 'I'm just glad it's worked out for you.'

The why-not-me pang that had kicked her in the teeth when he'd unexpectedly turned up on Friday seemed to have dissipated. All she felt now was genuine happiness on behalf of them both and a sense of tired resignation for herself. At least she was still in the running for her dream job. Any slip ups this weekend had mercifully not affected that. She latched onto that thought hard, and managed a smile.

He winked at her complete with clicking tongue.

'Just need to find yourself someone now, eh? You're exactly the same as ever – working when you should be having fun.' He put an arm around her shoulders and squeezed. 'Take a few risks, babe,' he said in her ear. 'Get out more.'

It was coming to something now she was actually receiving relationship advice from Luke-ex-commitment-phobic-Pemberton.

She watched him leave the hotel with his arm slung around Sabrina's tiny waist, the pair of them all smiles, and then she glanced down at her clipboard, on which were the details of next weekend's wedding festivities. A day off, and then she would be straight back into it.

Maybe Luke had a point.

CHAPTER 10

Four sets of property details in Amsterdam, any one of which would be the perfect location for his first European Loco bar, and Owen's enthusiasm was at an all-time low.

Amy Wilson stayed on his mind no matter how many hours he put in trying to distract himself, as if she'd somehow opened a door into a life of downtime and now his overworked body didn't want to close it again.

It wasn't just the fact she'd knocked him back. It was the way she'd made him *feel* about that. They were so alike. Wasn't part of the reason he was drawn to her at the outset because she prioritised work, just like he did? And her reason for turning him down, she'd said she didn't want to come second to his job, but what she was really saying was that he had no life. And with every day that passed, he'd found himself thinking more and more about his parents and his brother. Or about his friends, like Luke, who he no longer went out with because he had no time.

What was it she'd said – '*You're completely defined by your business, Owen. You are Loco. And deep down, I don't think you have room for anything else in your life.*'

She was right. He'd built a super-successful business from scratch without any help or support from his family. And just exactly how big a victory was that when he'd alienated everyone he could have shared it with? There was an entire side of his life missing and he only realised it now because he'd seen it in her, and recognised it as a waste.

He shoved the property details to one side of the desk and clicked open the cautiously chatty email from his brother, received nearly a month ago now.

Maybe it was time he finally replied.

'Could you possibly do something about that face before it curdles the White Russian?' Conrad said, waving a hand at the sample cocktail he was demonstrating.

'What the hell is that again?'

Amy really didn't care and only asked because he was so obviously dying to tell her. This new obsession with cocktail invention and encouragement of the young, hip and trendy to hang out at the Lavington's wine bar made her think of Mr Cocktail Bar himself, Owen Lloyd, who was undoubtedly proceeding with his one-man invasion of Europe. She'd heard nothing from him in six weeks, since she'd left his bedroom the night of Luke's wedding.

Not, of course, that she'd expected to.

'Vodka, coffee liqueur and a splash of cream over crushed ice,' Conrad said. 'We've got a feature coming up in one of the what's-on-in-London sections of the Sunday papers. I want our clientele to move away from pin-stripe fatcat businessmen making stopovers and more towards Made-In-Chelsea. Much younger and more fun demographic, darling.' He pointed at her with a swizzle stick. 'I'm planning on giving your cocktail bar boyfriend a run for his money.'

'He is NOT my boyfriend,' she said irritably.

Conrad raised an eyebrow.

'Whatever you say, darling.'

'He was too much like you,' she said. 'Too bloody interested in drinks to be really interested in me. Good work on the bar news though,' she conceded as a grumpy afterthought.

'You really need to get over this,' he said. '*You* turned *him* down, remember, not the other way around. You should be on top of the world. You landed the permanent Managerial post.'

Confirmation of her posting had admittedly brought a new high of self-satisfaction, which considering she'd been chasing it for virtually her entire working life had worn off extremely quickly. Where hard work and career goals had given her a sense of direction these past years, they now made her life feel one-sided, devoid of fun and excitement. All work and no play, as Owen had said. There he was, crashing her mind yet again.

'I am on top of the world,' she insisted. 'I made the right decision. I don't want my happiness in life to hinge on one expensive day or on someone else's commitment. I make my own happiness and security. That way I don't have to worry about someone else's opinion of me changing.'

Somehow it didn't sound as sensible as it used to, even when she said it out loud. Apparently Conrad felt the same because he rolled his eyes in a you're-talking-crap gesture.

'That's all very well, sweetie, as long as it's making you happy, but you've got a face like a slapped arse. What the hell is the point in having these mad life principles if all they do is make you miserable? You might as well take a risk if you're not happy anyway. Why don't you call him?'

'I don't have his number,' she blustered, because the thought of doing that filled her stomach with terrified excitement.

'Darling, he's not exactly Lord Lucan. He runs the most successful cocktail bar in Chelsea. Get yourself on the internet.'

Three days had passed since Conrad's pep talk, during which she'd actually morphed into a bit of a stalker.

Now she had her own tiny permanent office, complete with desktop computer, tracking Owen down was a five minute job. It was translating that into actually making a phone call that was holding her back.

Time after time she picked up the phone, only to drop it back in its cradle seconds later.

If he wanted to see me again he knows where I am.

She'd shot herself in the foot on that front when she'd told him she wasn't interested. Why would he get in touch after that? In three days she knew the phone numbers of all six of his bars. Maybe in another three days she might find the confidence to actually ring one of them. But what then? Was she really ready to get back out there and risk her heart at some point down the line?

A knock on the glass door of her office made her jump, followed by the receptionist poking her head around the door.

'Amy, someone to see you out in the lobby.'

She pressed escape madly to hide the fact that the browser was simultaneously open to three Owen Lloyd platforms - *Loco* Bar Facebook Page, a couple of reviews of his venue in Chelsea, and *Loco Ltd.'s* company website, complete with contact details through which she could, presumably with a couple of transfers, be connected to Owen Lloyd.

'Who is it?' she gabbled.

'Some kind of drinks salesman, I think. I tried to point him towards Conrad but he insisted on seeing you. Asked for you by name.'

Her heart plummeted through her stomach.

She nodded automatically, managerial smile pasted on her face. She pushed the chair back from her desk as if in a dream and headed out to the lobby.

Couldn't be him.

Was him.

It was late afternoon and the lobby bustled with people arriving to check in. A group of girls on a spa day were talking and laughing loudly on the sofas near the door. The concierge team trundled luggage across the marble floor. None of it registered in her consciousness.

Owen Lloyd wanted to see her again. He wore a dark blue shirt and jeans and his blue eyes had the same crease at the corners as he smiled at her. Her stomach performed circus-level cartwheels.

'Owen,' she said, cautiously professional, in case this visit wasn't about her at all and he wanted to book a sodding event or something.

'I wanted to see how you are,' he said lamely. 'I see you got the job. Congratulations.' He waved a hand around at the hotel.

It all felt so hideously stilted and awkward. What had he expected? That she might just fall into his arms?

'How's your invasion of Europe going? Have you found premises yet?'

Her voice was polite, no hint of the intimacy they'd shared. He took a deep breath. He hadn't come here to make some half-hearted stab at small talk. He'd come here to make her understand. At least then if she didn't want to give things a go, he could walk away knowing he'd given it his best shot.

'Can we go for a walk or something?' he said.

There was a pause, during which he was certain she would say she was far too busy. Then she glanced at her watch.

'I'm due a break,' she said.

They bought takeaway coffees from a stall in Hyde Park.

'I can't go too far,' she said. 'I need to get back fairly soon.'

The afternoon sun warmed his back. The park was green and open. It had been so long since he'd been anywhere like this. Even strolling felt alien to him, he was so used to rushing from one task to the next. Slowing down was a shock to the system.

'This won't take long,' he said.

'I thought you might be abroad,' she said. 'Viewing properties or something.'

Six weeks ago that had certainly been the plan.

'I'm taking some time, actually,' he said. 'It will be a massive personal commitment to take the *Loco* concept abroad, I'd pretty much have to put my life on hold.'

As if he had one.

'I want to make sure the bars in this country are properly established before I storm ahead. It *will* happen, I'm just…pacing myself a little.'

She smiled.

'That doesn't sound remotely like you.'

He didn't smile back. He wanted more than anything for her to see he was serious, that he wasn't here on some kind of a whim.

'I know. I think I may have reached a point where the bars have just saturated my whole life. When I came to Luke and Sabrina's wedding I was constantly on edge about taking time out. I'd begun to feel guilty about the slightest distraction from what I was doing.'

'Does that include me?'

Her tone was carefully guarded.

'No. Absolutely not.'

He glanced sideways at an empty bench, stopped walking and grabbed her free hand, tugging her to sit down next to him.

'Amy, listen.'

She looked at him, her brown eyes wide in her pretty face. Her lips were slightly parted and he fought the urge to kiss them. Instead he made do with keeping hold of her hand.

'The way I asked you out was totally crass, I can see that now. I was just so afraid of letting anyone get close, of distracting me from the business. When I was with you that weekend it was the first time in I don't know how long that my mind wasn't constantly on work.'

She nodded slowly. 'OK.'

'You have to understand, I gave up so much to follow my own path, and I don't mean missing out on the opportunity to run a dairy farm. Giving that up was the easy part. It was how that made my family feel that was the real problem. We were so close, and I ripped that to bits. I felt so resentful that they weren't prepared to be supportive of my ideas and they felt hurt that I apparently just dismissed everything they'd worked for. We barely spoke for three years, everything was so awkward between us. And because of that I had to make the business work, do you see? I had to prove to them that I hadn't just ruined our family on a stupid whim. I had to prove it to myself too so that maybe the guilt would go away.' He shrugged. 'I may have got a bit caught up in that. The business ended up becoming my whole life. I worked seven-day weeks, I didn't do relationships. Hell, I barely did friendships – anything that I thought detracted from my goals. I even resented Luke for asking me to be his best man, because it meant taking time out from work. I didn't spend any time organising his stag night, I cobbled together a last-minute speech. I was a pretty crap friend when you get right down to it.'

'When I met you and saw how much you wanted that kind of family support, the kind I'd screwed up, it made me think about my parents for once. They'd tried to get back in touch this last year or so but I was having none of it. I just couldn't let go of that guilt and resentment. I thought it was easier to delete their phone messages and emails than to actually address things. But really I was missing out on so much because I was too proud to apologise or make amends. I just poured everything into work and didn't let anything in my personal life interfere with that.'

He sighed.

'And that's why when I asked you out to dinner I ended up doing it in such a crappy half-hearted way. I don't blame you for running a mile. I didn't exactly make you feel special, did I – suggesting you fit in around work?'

She shook her head.

'No, but it wasn't exactly a surprise.' She took a sip of her coffee, looking out across the green lawn of the park. The air was fresh and sweet. It was lovely to be outside for a while. 'I've spent a long time feeling like I'm second best or not quite good enough. I think I'd actually *assumed* I would have come second to your job. I know it started with Roger of course, when I was seven I thought if I'd been better behaved or done better at school then

93

maybe he would have stayed, which is utter crap of course. But somehow that feeling has managed to stay on. It's only now, after seeing Luke again, meeting you, that I see how *much* I've been making that assumption ever since. Not just with you but with everything.

'With Luke for example, I assumed it was down to some failing of *mine* that he only wanted to settle down when he met someone else. But I was never right for him at all. And then with work, I thought being passed over for the top job was down to my never quite being good enough but in reality, looking back, it was more about me lacking in confidence despite the fact I'm perfectly capable. I've been so quick to see everything with a glass-half-empty attitude that I've let it take over my life. I pre-empt anything I think might go wrong for me and then let that affect how I behave. You included.'

She looked at him apologetically.

'I was certain dating you would be doomed, that I'd be heart-broken within weeks or months. So I didn't even give it a try. It's only since you left that I realised I felt bloody miserable anyway. What was the point? I was supposed to be saving myself grief, not bringing it on.'

She half-expected this conversation to be over now he knew what a negative nightmare she could be. Instead a tiny leap of excitement in her chest as he put an arm around her. She leaned her head against his shoulder.

We're both as bad as each other,' he said. 'Come out for dinner with me. Sod work. Sod everything. I want to make a go of this.'

Her heart melted.

He nodded across the park. Joggers, families picnicking, mothers pushing strollers.

'Look at all these people having a life. I think it's time we got one.'

She tilted her head up and smiled at him as he smoothed her hair back from her face and kissed her.

'Sounds like a plan,' she said.